breaking
BETH

Jennifer Bene

ISBN (e-book): 978-1-946722-21-8

ISBN (paperback): 978-1-946722-38-6

Cover design by Laura Hidalgo, Beyond DEF Lit. https://www.beyonddeflit.com/

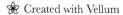 Created with Vellum

Instead of a dedication for this book, which would just feel strange, I have a quick little letter for you all instead. Please read it on the next pages and be sure you want to dive into this story before you get too far in to turn back.

And remember, I adore you either way, lovelies.

A Note To My Lovely Readers

Hello lovelies,

I wanted to start this book with a quick note, just so no one is blindsided, or buys it and later regrets it. This is a dark story, and I know you're probably chuckling to yourself because *all* of my stories are pretty dark, or at least edgy and dirty. But Beth? Beth is unlike anything else I've published. If you've read the Thalia series you will have a greater appreciation for this book (if you haven't, I do recommend it because this book will spoil a few surprises from Book 1).

In fact, the spoilers are about to start, so… run away. Run away now if you don't want them!

Are they gone? *Okay.*

Beth's name originally appeared in 'Security Binds Her' where she was referenced by Marcus as another girl that had been trained by his brother Anthony — and, let's just say that based on their conversation things did *not* go well. From the first moment I referenced Beth, I think there was a little spark of bloody darkness in the back of my mind that wanted to know exactly what happened to her. What horrific things did Anthony do that made even Marcus quail?

Fast forward three years and Addison Cain, Cari Silverwood, and I were chatting one day about how people flinch at the things we put in our books sometimes... but we all admitted that we often hold back. We *rein ourselves in* with most of our books, and usually cut or never write some of the more fucked up stuff that we come up with. Thus was born the idea to have a 'chains off' anthology. No rules, no limits, no chains on our internal demons. Even as we were joking and laughing about everything we could do with our options wide open, I already knew what I wanted to write.

I wanted to write the story of Beth and Anthony.

Let me be very clear, this is not a love story. It is a walk into a deep, dark fucking cave where the only thing that happens is the light of the entrance shrinking ever smaller at your back while you keep trudging forward. Everyone that read this when it originally appeared in the 'When the Dark Wins' anthology has told me that by the end they felt gutted, emptied out, and basically depressed. Cari described it as 'bottom of the grave dark, after the dirt's filled in'. There is no happy ending here, lovelies, there is no 'happy for now' — there is *no happy*. This is a story about hope dying, about coming face to face with a psychopath and losing (or winning by losing, depending on your perspective).

Now, 'Breaking Beth' _will_ be followed by a duet of books that are a much more traditional dark romance about finding the right person and being healed. While I hope to write those books in such a way that this book isn't required, it will always be the dark and fucked up first part of the rest of Beth's story, and I love you for trusting me enough to read it.

It will not be an easy read, but I do hope you enjoy it, lovelies. It's for the truly dark hearted among us, or those who just have to know what happened to Beth.

Love you all,

Jennifer
Bene

ONE

Anthony

———————

"Is the girl situated?" Glancing up from his phone, Anthony caught the flush in Marcus' cheeks. It was either arousal or simple exertion — *he'd always had trouble telling the two apart* — but it didn't matter. He didn't care what his brother was feeling or not feeling.

"Yeah, she's in there."

"Secured?" he asked, and Marcus shoved his hand through his hair, gripping it at the back where it was just long enough to do so. The silence between them lingered. "Was that a complicated question?"

"Fuck off," Marcus snapped, stomping away from the bedroom, and Anthony sighed. Short-tempered and shortsighted, his little brother clearly needed to be coddled again.

His least favorite activity.

Following at a leisurely pace, he finished his email reply and then tucked the phone away in his pocket. Marcus was already pouring a glass of whiskey when he found him in the office.

So weak. So pathetic.

But… he had his uses.

"Was there an issue acquiring her that I should be aware of?" Anthony waited as Marcus knocked back the whiskey and poured another.

"Of course not, I knew where to get her. It was simple."

"Then would you care to answer my question?" Anthony sighed when Marcus muttered obscenities under his breath. "If you need me to secure her because you did not, tell me now so I can go handle it."

"She's tied down, collar on, but I'm telling you my method is better. If you'd just fucking *let* me, I could make her like it." Another grumbled curse as Marcus licked the whiskey from his bottom lip, an irritated sigh escaping. "You won't even have a chance to talk to her when she wakes up terrified. She'll just start screaming."

"Oh, I know she will." A smile tugged at the edge of his lips, and he couldn't ignore the buzz in his blood that the idea inspired. The only highs in his life came from those screams, and the crying and begging that would follow.

Everything in-between those brief moments of suffering was just so much… *white noise*.

"How can you expect to train her when she won't even listen to you?"

"They always listen to pain, Marcus." Tilting his head, he met his brother's eyes. "Eventually."

"Pleasure works faster."

"And did you *pleasure* this new one?" The mockery in his tone was unavoidable.

Marcus' greatest weakness was his lust. Lust for physical intimacy, lust for gaining positive responses from the slaves, and mostly his lust to finally come out on top and be better than him at something.

Unlikely.

Anthony had been taking and training slaves for years and bringing in his brother had simply been good business. The man had an eye for natural submissives, which made the process somewhat easier. He was loyal, and he was an excellent delivery boy. But it would be *better* for business if Marcus would stop thinking with his prick and viewing the slaves as anything other than commodities.

There was an odd look on his brother's face as they watched each other, some mixture of irritation with him and hunger for the girl. Not like it fazed him either way. But it promised an argument that Anthony did not want to entertain.

After all, the girl could wake up at any moment and he wanted to watch her panic. To listen to those first desperate sounds, her first screams.

"You know you're not supposed to fuck them when you take them." Anthony pressed his buttons, and Marcus slammed his glass down as if on cue.

"I didn't fuck her! I caught her, drugged her, and brought her here." Thrusting his hand in the vague direction of the bedroom, he continued, "And then I *secured* her for you."

"Good. Then you can get back to whatever you had planned." Anthony pulled out his phone again, wanting the cameras on in time for the wake up.

The customers liked the first screams too.

"We just sold the last one, Anthony, we could have waited another week." He shook his head, swallowing another mouthful of alcohol as if it could make him not feel whatever odd emotions he harbored.

Fortunately, Anthony had never had to deal with trivial things like guilt or pity. They had simply never been a part of him, and why should they be? Emotions were distractions.

Flaws.

Especially when there were so many things he could do to their new product. So many ways to make her scream, to break her down. Options unrolled in front of him like a luxurious, blood red carpet, diverting his attention from Marcus' clear disquiet.

He needed to end this discussion so he could be there when she awoke and her confusion slowly turned to fear.

It would be exquisite.

"I'm still trying to get the house set up, we didn't need to grab Beth yet." Marcus' fingers twitched against the edge of the glass, an old tell that telegraphed his needs even better than the wobble of his voice when he spoke her name.

Pathetic.

Ignoring his sibling's inconstant emotions, Anthony flicked

on the cameras from his control panel and watched as the feminine shape appeared against the darker sheets.

Marcus kept talking as if he hadn't heard him. "Her name is Beth. Elizabeth Doherty."

"Do you have any *useful* information that I didn't already find in my research?" He tapped away on his phone, sending out the alerts that a new event was live. "Anything relevant, or are you stalling so you can continue to chug my Van Winkle's Reserve 20-year bourbon like an animal?"

Marcus sighed heavily. "She's strong willed, fought the drugs longer than I expected. Everything else you already know."

Anthony made a sound at the back of his throat, but otherwise didn't acknowledge the unintentional compliment. Flipping back to the camera screen, he saw her stretched out and vulnerable against the bedding. Already so much different from her smiling driver's license photo. In time he would erase that person completely. "You can go now," Anthony dismissed him as he turned out of the office to walk towards the bedroom.

"Why don't you let me have her first? I can get her to understand her situation. Accept it." The grating sound of Marcus' voice followed him as he watched the girl twitch in her sleep.

She would wake up soon.

"Don't you have a house to set up? Another girl to track? It was your idea to start running two operations." And at least then Marcus' whining would be a state away.

"I thought I should be here to—"

"Your assistance is unnecessary." Pulling his eyes from the screen, he saw the tension in his brother's jaw, a muscle ticking as he avoided eye contact. "What is it, Marcus? Do you think I'm going to hurt her?"

As soon as he smiled, Marcus growled and flipped him off, turning back towards the front of the house. "I know exactly what you're going to do."

"Really? I like to think I'm quite inventive." The camera angle switched, and he watched as her body shifted.

"I'm going, Anthony. I'll be back in a couple of days." Marcus spoke from the end of the hall, and he glanced up without another word. Goodbyes were for people who thought he was human, and Marcus had lost that illusion before he was six.

It was better that Marcus was leaving. The last girl had broken so easily, and then she had cried for Marcus like he would help her just because he liked to make them orgasm. He hadn't helped her, of course, but it had been irritating all the same. When Anthony made girls scream, he wanted them to beg *him* for mercy.

Even though it would never come.

TWO

Anthony

Anthony sat at the foot of the bed, leaning back in his chair and working through the backlog of emails he'd been ignoring as he waited for the girl to wake up. Customers with requests, questions, and now he was able to answer them.

Yes, there is a new slave.

A new girl to watch, to bring in more customers, to feed their needs, and that always meant more money. It was nice to have a job doing something he enjoyed.

His customers were mere shadows of men who did not have the fortitude to make their wishes a reality. Too afraid of repercussions, of their own weakness. But they had always paid well for the privilege of watching him work.

The girl twitched on the bed, her legs pulling against the ropes that held her thighs wide. It was entrancing, the way the rope dug into her skin, already red and inflamed from her unconscious efforts, and he wondered for a moment just how hard she'd fight them.

He thought about slapping her. As close to consciousness as she was, it would rouse her immediately — but then he wouldn't get to watch her hope die slowly.

Better to be patient, to *wait*.

Something Marcus never understood, and likely never would. There was so much more to enjoy in this process beyond the physical, and he wanted to take his time. To destroy her slowly, devour every inch of her mind. To strangle it until her awareness was focused into a pinpoint of what her Master demanded of her.

A quiet groan and the girl tried to turn, her arms and legs pulling in unison as she attempted to curl up. Finally, her eyes opened, her breath caught, and Anthony found his own breath had stilled in his lungs as he put his phone away to enjoy every minute of her devastation.

Showtime.

She gasped, her head rolling to look at the rope wrapped around her wrist as he stayed completely still, completely silent. Enjoying the way her knees lifted from the bed as she discovered the restraints. Her breathing picked up, panic setting in as she whined and pulled harder at the ropes. When she tried to sit up the collar tethered to the headboard stopped her short, but she saw him.

More silence.

The girl was exactly what he'd needed. Blonde, toned, tanned. Practically mail order from the requests of the customers. Her brown eyes were wide, and more than anything Anthony wished he could hear the scattered thoughts tumbling through her mind.

That would be entertaining.

"Hello," Anthony spoke, breaking the spell, and she whined louder. Her body contorted, dropping back to the bed as she twisted uselessly against the ropes. From his vantage point her struggles were quite lovely, thighs spreading, hips working at empty air, but it was her sheer panic that flavored it perfectly.

"Oh my God — this isn't — *no...*" Lifting her head she looked at him, and he met her gaze calmly, leaning forward in the chair. Then her ribs expanded just before her first scream ripped free. "HELP! SOMEONE PLEASE HELP ME!"

"No one can hear you," he told her, but his words didn't register yet.

"PLEASE! HELP! SOMEONE!" Jerking violently off the bed, she twisted again, and Anthony just watched as her skin rubbed raw against the rope. He wasn't concerned about her getting loose. Despite their conflicting beliefs, Marcus was excellent with knots. She wasn't getting free.

She was *never* getting free — she just didn't know it yet.

Another panicked, desperate scream sent blood rushing to his cock, but he ignored it. There was plenty of time for that. Patience was the thing that Marcus lacked. A year of working with him and he'd yet to understand that the best tool available was the slave's own mind. Allowing them to torture themselves before the *real* fun began... that was how you broke them.

The girl, *Beth*, sagged against the bed, breath whistling in her lungs as she turned her head and relentlessly worked at her bonds. He waited for her to come to terms with her situation — naked, tied-down, spread wide. Eventually, she lifted her head and met his eyes again. Round, brown, tear-soaked orbs in a pretty face.

She would make them money for sure.

"Who are you? Why am I here? Why me? Why?" Beth's voice trembled, a little raspy from the dry mouth he expected after the sedative. Almost every girl asked the same questions in their own ways, so many *whys*, and it brought him that fizzy feeling of what others called 'joy' to answer her.

"I'm your Master, and you're here to be trained so I can sell you." He hadn't even finished speaking before she screamed again. A long, screeching wail that buzzed over his skin, making his cock rock hard in his pants.

"No, no, no, no…" she pleaded to the ceiling, her head rocking back and forth on the mattress as she unconsciously contracted her limbs against the ropes again.

"And you were chosen because you were what we needed."

"NO!" Her shout was raw, breaking her voice, but he only tilted his head as he watched her. There was a moment where she became aware of his vantage point, her thighs trying to pull together to meet, but the bed was too wide for that. Her shaved cunt was on display for him, and for everyone watching on the cameras.

Which is what they paid for.

"Do you want to know what is going to happen to you?" he taunted her with the question, and her next groan halted in her chest as she licked her lips. Fear almost tangible in the air between them.

"Are… are you going to rape me?" The delicious trepidation in her question had his cock twitching.

"Not yet," he answered, and she dropped back to the bed, a choked sob escaping her as she wrestled with the ropes that gave her no more room than his brother had allowed her. It was a pretty sight, and part of him hoped Marcus had signed into the feed on his drive North so he could enjoy the fruits of his labors.

"Let me go, please, I swear—"

"You won't tell anyone? Go to the police? Etcetera, etcetera?" Anthony felt a smile on his lips as he leaned forward, her head lifting to meet his gaze. "Haven't you realized you're not going anywhere? That you won't be *able* to tell anyone anything?"

"FUCK YOU!" she screamed, and her back arched off the bed as she did, her breasts angled towards the cameras in the ceiling.

"Later. There's more to discuss first, *Beth*." It was irritating to use her name, things didn't have names, but he needed her attention. And it would take time to truly make her a thing, but he would. He always did.

"You can't do this! You can't — you…" She trailed off as the panic overtook her again. People were so fragile, their minds so narrow in their capacity to absorb concepts they didn't want to. The girl was property now, nothing more than a body, and it was his job to break her mind *just* enough that she was pliable. Like making dough, he would knead her into the proper shape, beat her if necessary, all so she could rise to her new purpose.

"It's already done. The sooner you accept your place, the

better it will be for you. Though I must admit, I enjoy the slaves who fight."

"NO!" she screamed again, and he felt the vibrations of the air down to his core, wrapping around his spine to make him shiver with the closest thing to delight he was capable. The girl was better than he had hoped, and he pushed himself out of the chair to stand at his full height. He was a tall man. Over six feet. And to a slender girl tied spread-eagle on a strange mattress, he knew it felt like twenty when he loomed over her. It was all about perspective. He worked out, wore suits, kept up appearances — all to maintain the image — but he knew that as aesthetically pleasing as he might be, there was no way to hide the creature under the surface.

At some point he had just ceased trying to appear human.

Others like him, and he had met many, worked hard to hide what they were, to suppress their urges to do the worst to other people. The money coming in every month from their little operation was proof enough of that, but as he stood beside the bed and looked into her face, he could tell that she wanted comfort. Wanted him to hide his true self for just a moment. Provide a glimpse of some humanity in the man standing over her, something to kindle hope, give her the glimmer of a light at the end of the tunnel.

That old, childish lie of *'everything is going to be okay'*.

It wouldn't be. Not for her, anyway. Anthony would quite enjoy the things he was going to do to her.

"Are you afraid?" he asked, his voice as steady and calm as it always was.

"What?!" she screeched, but he doubted even she was so stupid as to misunderstand a question that simple.

Regardless, she *was* afraid. He could see it in her. She broadcasted her fear at top volume, muscles jumping, palms sweating, bound hands clenching and unclenching... but he wanted to hear it. "Are you afraid?" he asked again, maintaining the cold edge in his tone.

"I— *yes*..." she finally whispered the word, a hushed and broken sound that made his cock strain against his zipper.

"Describe it for me."

"I don't understand."

"Tell me what the fear feels like." His first touch to the skin along her ribs made her jerk, pulse jumping at her throat, face turned away like she could avoid him. Eventually she would realize how pointless it was, and so he enjoyed it while he could. Soaked in her panic, watched the hope dim just a little inside her as he sat down on the edge of the bed. "Just describe it."

He wasn't sure he'd ever felt fear. There had been plenty of times when he was aware of danger, more than once that he'd felt physical pain and known more was coming. But there was no surging heartbeat beyond the requirements of his body, no flash of something *more* in the vacuum inside him.

But she was feeling it, real fear, and he wanted to know what it felt like.

Moving his hand to her stomach he spread out his fingers, almost covering her taut abdomen as her muscles spasmed. "I'm waiting."

"It feels like fear, what the FUCK do you want from me?" she shouted the question, the vibrations of her voice coming up through his fingertips just before he dug them into her skin. A whine of pain, her face contorting with it, but this was just the beginning. She would learn new levels of pain and realize that the way he pressed his nails into her skin was gentle. An introduction, a graceful easing in.

"Let me help. Is your heart racing?" As he asked, he relaxed his hand and moved it upward, between her breasts to graze her throat. The rapid pounding of her blood just under her skin was answer enough, but he wanted her to voice it. "Speak."

"*Yes.*" Another weak-voiced concession from her soft lips.

He tightened his grip on her throat ever so slightly, just enough to threaten the airway. "And are you breathing faster?" he prompted.

The girl swallowed, the swell of it pressing against his palm. "I don't want to die," she whispered, tears brimming at the edges of her eyes, and he smiled.

It was his smile that pushed her into the first sob. Marcus had always told him there was something wrong with his smile — he could never do it right. But it had barely been ten minutes and they had already had so many firsts. A scream, a touch, half-moon marks embedded in her stomach, and then a sob. She was rushing things, making it difficult to savor each of them separately.

And look, now the first tears.

He ran his thumb up her cheek, catching one before he lifted his hand from her skin. Wide eyes watched him, pupils dilating as her autonomic nervous system kicked her into fight or flight. The slick moisture made his fingers rub together smoothly, and for a flash he wondered if her cunt were just as slick.

Could she be as excited by their interaction as he was?

It was unlikely, but Marcus usually chose well. The pain would summon a reaction from her and he couldn't wait to find out what it was.

"It's good that you don't want to die. A strong survival instinct will help you to make smart choices." Anthony wiped his hand on his pants, clearing her tears away. "And killing you would be such a waste."

"You won't kill me?"

He couldn't help but smile again. "What fun would that be?"

"Oh God!" Another wail, and the tears were back as she pulled at the rope, ripping at her skin in her panic. Anthony watched her for a moment, imagining what that fear must feel like. Taste like. Was it coppery like blood? Bitter like a lemon?

Or was it as sweet for her as it was for him? Lush and rich like a sinful dessert.

The girl had done such a poor job of describing it and, if it would work, he would cut her open just to see the fear. To feel it like she did, if just for a moment. But… that wasn't possible. There was no way to experience what she felt, he could only see his side of the equation, and at least he could enjoy *this*.

"Oh my God, this can't be happening," she whined.

"Do you think your God is listening?" Anthony tilted an

ear towards the ceiling as if he were waiting to hear an answer from the heavens. "Do you think he will save you?"

Her body shook, she was biting back the sobs that made her ribs quake. From somewhere inside her she summoned the strength to meet his eyes and he respected the effort it took. "What do you want from me?" she asked, her voice cracking again.

"Everything." Reaching out he stroked her cheek, and then caught her chin when she tried to turn away, fingers digging into the bone as he made her face him. "And I will have it."

THREE

Beth

———————

This had to be a nightmare.

Things like this didn't happen in real life.

Beth closed her eyes as the man finally released her chin, and she tucked it against her chest, trying to wipe away his touch — as useless as the effort was. She knew he was still standing beside the bed, in a tailored suit that probably cost more than the rent for her shitty apartment in Santa Rosa. She could tell from the elegantly sterile room, and from the man standing over her, that he had enough money to do whatever he had planned.

Another sob threatened to choke her airway, but his eyes glinted whenever she cried. He clearly enjoyed it, and that meant she needed to stop.

Her head was just too damn fuzzy, her mouth too dry, and it was making it hard to think. The ropes around her wrists and ankles, combined with whatever was around her neck, only made it worse. She wished this could be a nightmare, that when she opened her eyes she'd be home. Safe and sound. Laughing about her ridiculous nightmare as she took the stopper out of a bottle of wine and poured until she forgot his cold blue eyes.

But it wasn't a nightmare.

She knew that.

Which was why opening her eyes and finding him there wasn't a surprise, but it did make something ache deep inside. He stared at her like a bug under glass, held down with pins instead of ropes. There was something *off* about him, more than just the fact that he'd taken her.

He didn't feel… real, although his touch definitely had. It made her skin crawl, made her want to pull away even though the restraints made that impossible.

What do you want from me?

Everything.

The word echoed inside her like a funeral dirge. He'd implied that he wouldn't kill her because it wasn't *fun*, but when he was done with her she wondered if she wouldn't wish for death.

"You can let me go." She found enough of a voice to speak the words softly, as if she were speaking to a wild animal, but the way he looked at her answered her plea before he'd even spoken.

"That would be a waste of effort," he replied. Almost robotic. That strange, cold tone remaining in his voice even as he stood and walked away from her towards a doorway that she guessed to be a bathroom. The sound of running water confirmed it, and she desperately pulled at the ropes again, even though her skin tingled and burned as she struggled.

He returned to her with a glass and the sandpaper scratch of her throat urged her to lift her head so he could press it against her lips. "Drink," he commanded.

All of her panicked breathing had dried her mouth. The first wash of clean water on her tongue almost made her choke, but she managed to swallow. Again, and again, feeling the cool rush hitting her empty stomach, waking up the hunger she'd ignored in her terror.

Dinner.

She had missed dinner because she had never made it home after work — but when had he taken her? Turning her head away from the glass, she swallowed and tried to focus on her blurry memories. The evening hadn't felt any different from a normal one. She had walked towards her car, parked in the public lot like it always was, and then... *nothing.*

Nothing except waking up in this godforsaken bed, with the devil sitting at the foot.

Only now the devil was holding a half-full glass of water, staring down at her like some science experiment.

"Who are you?" she asked, speaking easier now that her mouth wasn't a desert.

"Your current Master. You should try out the word, get used to it."

"No." Beth felt her nails pricking her palms as she balled them into fists again, but her answer only seemed to entertain him.

He placed the water glass on the bedside table before he walked to a long poster on the wall across from the bed. Resting a hand near the second line, he pointed at it: *You will address me as Master. Everyone else as Sir or Ma'am.*

As hard as it was to focus, she tried to read the long list, but the first one drew her attention and kept it. It was as sterile as he seemed to be, and just as terrifying.

You are not your own. You are property.

"I'm not property," she argued.

"You are. You just haven't accepted it yet, but I will help you understand." That odd curve of his lips happened again, something she might call a smile on anyone else — but not on him. When he did it, it wasn't a smile, it was something more sinister. Like an animal baring teeth before it tore your throat out.

"I don't want to understand. I want to go home!" Beth tried to make her voice strong, to make it as decisive and calm and collected as his, but there was still a tremor when she said the word home. A flash of her mom, her dad, her sister and brother and their families. Her two-year-old nephew. It weakened her, made her shudder, and so she tried to push them away as his fingers drummed against the poster.

There were weapons, tools, on the walls on either side of the list, and she knew without asking that they were meant for her.

She wanted to be brave as he lifted his hand from the phrases, taking a few steps before plucking a long metal thing from the wall. Two prongs loomed at the end, and when he wrapped his hands around the base a loud, electric *snap* crackled through the room.

Fuck no.

"I prefer to give you the rules up front, then you'll know exactly why you're being punished if you disobey one." Casually, he walked towards her, resting the terrifying thing on the bed beside her leg. Shrugging out of the suit jacket, he dropped it into his chair and then worked at the cuffs of his dress shirt. Unbutton, roll-up sleeve. Repeat.

Never breaking eye contact as he prepared to hurt her.

"Please don't do this." There was no strength in her voice as he picked up the tool and the bright flash from its tip was accompanied by another loud crackle of electricity. Her body jerked involuntarily, terror rolling through her.

A cattle prod. That's a fucking cattle prod.

The name of it registered, even though the knowledge was useless.

"You can keep begging." He trailed the twin prongs at the tip down her thigh and she whined, waiting for the pain. "But read the first rule aloud."

Lifting her head once more she stared at the stark black letters, but her mouth wouldn't form them. *I'm not property. I'm a person.*

This can't be happening.

Sudden, blinding pain zapped her thigh, the pop of the cattle prod firing almost lost in her involuntary yelp. It had been quick, sharp torment, and now the muscle was sore beneath it, the skin tingling. The man sighed, eyes narrowing slightly as he looked her over before he met her gaze. "I do not enjoy repeating myself, that is another lesson you can learn from this. Now, read."

The cattle prod touched the inside of her other thigh and Beth jumped. "You— you are n-not your own, you are property."

"Good. Now read it in the first person, not the second. I want to hear you acknowledge the words." He tilted his head towards the wall, prompting her unnecessarily. "Go on, slave. *I am not…*"

Clenching her jaw, Beth bit back the tears as he called her *slave* again. What had she done to deserve this? Why had he picked her? This was—

The sharp stab of electricity on the delicate skin of her inner thigh forced a scream. It ripped out of her, straining her throat, her legs trying to close. To protect herself.

Impossible.

The fucking metal prongs slid higher on her inner thigh and panic owned her completely as she shouted out the words he wanted. "I'm not my own! I'm property! THERE! Just stop, please don't."

"Was that so hard?" he asked, a smile that was not a smile on his lips. When she only glared at him, he dug the points of the prod into her skin, pressing until they hurt all on their own, his cold smile never faltering. "Second rule."

Beth swallowed, looking at the poster again. "I can't do this, I can't be a slave, I swear this—"

Somewhere, someone was screaming. It wasn't until the too-loud sputter of electricity stopped that she realized it was her. She'd never heard her own voice like that. It sounded like someone dying, and he watched her with fascination as she gasped for air. Eyes never wavering, not even a hint of temper, just a serene *enjoyment* of her suffering. "By all means, continue disobeying me. If you pass out from the pain, I'll just wake you up so we can finish."

He's insane.

She was tied down to a bed in front of an insane man holding a fucking cattle prod. Skin burning, muscles twitching, she wrapped her hands around the ropes like they could help her. "I will address you as…"

"Yes?" The cattle prod moved to her hip, just on the inside of the bone. Normally, she was terribly ticklish there. Even the brush of a finger could have her collapsing into giggles, but nothing happened. Fear and pain made the idea of laughing impossible.

"I will address you as Master." *Never.* "Everyone else as Sir or Ma'am…" She swallowed as the words sunk in. "Are there really others here?" *Others like him?* Just the idea had her stomach turning as he moved the metal tips in tiny circles on her skin.

"Not right now," he answered, and then his eyes slid down her body, landing between her thighs. "Keep going."

"I will kneel in all rooms, and again whenever you enter." Licking her lips, she twitched with the urge to deny every word leaving her lips. *I'm just reading, I'm not agreeing. These are all lies. Lies, lies, lies.*

"Do you need me to prompt you?" The man's ice blue eyes glinted just before the pain hit. A shorter burst than before, but it felt worse on her stomach. She could taste blood in her mouth as awareness returned. One side of her tongue ached as she whimpered and tried to blink the tears from her eyes to read.

Just get it over with.

"I will crawl when told to follow. I will ask permission to speak, to ask a question, to—"

The man's smile widened as he dragged the dangerous metal across her lower belly, and then he adjusted his hold on the controls and pressed the tips against her folds.

"Oh, God, no, no! It says orgasm, it says ask permission to orgasm!" Beth tried to pull away from the prod, heels digging into the mattress, hands pulling on the ropes, but she couldn't move more than an inch, and that inch was painful. Pulse pounding in the blood trapped in her feet. It didn't matter anyway, he continued stroking her with the fucking cattle prod, grazing her clit, but there was no pleasure. There would be no pleasure here, and she knew that. His eyes were empty. Two hollow, icy caves. "Do you honestly think I'll orgasm?"

"It happens sometimes." The flippant response was just a confirmation, as if orgasms happened on accident. As if she might stumble into one and have to apologize. *He's psychotic.* "It will be extraordinarily painful if I pull the trigger right now, slut."

Her fear ratcheted up another notch, and she scrambled to speak, "I— I will wear no clothing, unless you provide it."

"That's right, although that one is more for whomever I sell you to. If you could find clothes in this house, I'd be quite impressed." He removed the prod from between her legs and she sagged against the mattress in relief... until he brushed it across a nipple. Poking at the tightening bud with one of the prongs. She felt frozen as she watched, breath held in her lungs. A *tsk'ing* sound left him, but she opened her mouth too late.

The bright flash nearly blinded her, so close to her face as she snapped back from the wash of agony. Crying, screaming, cursing, she tried to blink away the multi-colored blotches in her vision.

"Slave, I will put the cattle prod away as soon as you read the last two rules."

FOUR

Anthony
_____

The girl had read the final two lines of the poster at such a panicked pace that he couldn't help but be a little proud of how quickly she'd come around.

Cattle prods could do that though… when it came to slaves electricity was always effective.

Red blotches bloomed on her skin from the places he'd struck, but they would heal quickly. Never helpful to mar the merchandise. The customers wanted to watch because she was pretty. One of them would buy her because they liked to look at her. Ruining that for his own fun would be pointless.

She was crying quietly on the bed, cursing under her breath. Likely cursing *him*.

Not like he cared.

The glare she'd given him after he'd shocked her other breast promised that the fire wasn't out inside her. *Yet*. But he had wanted to even out the color on her small chest. To make them match, and to hear her scream again, because this one screamed so prettily.

As he replaced the cattle prod on the wall, he contemplated hurting her for breaking the second to last rule: *You will thank your Master for all punishments.*

But... it hadn't truly been a punishment. More of a painful educational session. And he was always honest with the slaves about his expectations, and the consequences for disobeying. There were other ways of making her suffer tonight anyway.

The heavy strain of his cock was uncomfortably distracting now, and that meant it was time to reward his patience and give her a different kind of lesson.

Returning to the bed he appreciated how she flinched, already associating his presence with pain. Which was exactly as it *should* be. She needed to accept who was in charge, accept who held all the power, and the next step of their first evening together would illustrate that perfectly.

Anthony sat down beside her again, tracing the welt near her hipbone. Her eyes were squeezed tight, possibly trying to ignore his touch, possibly trying to obey the last rule: *You will keep your eyes down at all times unless directed.* But he liked the way her brown eyes glistened with tears, and that meant he wanted them open.

"Look at me," he commanded, and she obeyed instantly. Eyelids snapping open as she panted, pulse flickering in her neck just below the collar. "Good."

"I can't... I can't do this," she whispered.

"You'd be surprised what you're capable of surviving." His words sounded comforting to his own ears, but her chest jerked with a sob that she managed to suppress. Such a pretty sight, tear-streaked and tied down. Moving his hand lower he brushed between her thighs and she whined, eyes clenched tight again. "Eyes," he corrected, and they opened.

Obedience was its own drug, but the fix wasn't enough.

There was strength in her she wasn't even aware of yet, a challenge for him to push against, to see just how much she *could* take before she broke and was no longer interesting.

Dragging his middle finger between her folds he watched her face, fear making her shake. Her cunt wasn't wet, which was slightly disappointing, but perhaps she didn't respond well to electricity.

There were other things to try. *Tomorrow*.

Pushing his finger inside her brought the sweetest sound from her lips. Desolate and resigned. Another piece of her hope dying right before his eyes.

It was going to be wonderful to chip away even more of it as he fucked her.

Removing his hand, he stood and took off his belt, the *swish* of the shiny leather leaving his belt loops made her cry again. "Please, no…" she whispered, and he almost groaned.

He did enjoy this part. They were never quite as timorous after the first time, because they knew what it felt like to be violated.

This would be special. Memorable.

Dropping the belt in the chair, he moved it aside so he could put a knee on the bed between her spread legs. She pulled against the ropes as he climbed up, angling his body over hers so she could recognize the futility of her efforts. "You do look lovely when you cry and scream. I think it will make you quite popular."

She didn't respond, jaw clenched tight, breath shuddering in and out of her nose, but her quiet defiance wouldn't last long.

Sitting up, he opened the button on his slacks, lowering the zipper before he pushed it all out of the way so he could grasp his cock. Her whimper was perfectly timed with the first stroke of his fingers over the sensitive head, like she was teasing him. "You're not wet, but I'm feeling gracious after your efforts with the rules… so, I'll make you a deal."

Leaning forward he braced one hand beside her ribs, brushing his other against her cheek. She jerked her head away, but he only smiled.

"I'll let you spit into my hand, but that will be the only lubricant you'll get." Offering his hand, he watched as she glanced at it and then met his gaze again.

"Go to hell," she hissed, punctuating the damnation by spitting into his face. Barely a spray, which wouldn't have made what was coming next any easier, but it couldn't go unanswered.

"You're really going to regret that." Anthony sat up and slapped her, her gasp dissolving into angry tears as she yanked at her wrists and bucked her hips off the bed. *A fighter.* His cock pulsed, and he felt the urge to take her amplifying. It was as much a lesson in power at this point as it was to sate his own needs.

The girl wasn't aroused, and as he wiped his face clean of

her spittle and stroked his cock with the meager offering she'd made, he knew this would be uncomfortable for both of them at first, but he was willing to deal with it.

Sacrifices must be made.

Lowering his hips between her spread thighs, he lined up with her cunt and thrust hard. He groaned, she yelped. It burned a little, physical sensation skittering across his nerves as he drew back and forced himself further in, feeling her body yield under his strength. There was no stopping this. It had been inevitable since her name had appeared on their list. This was just the glorious culmination of their careful planning. The reward.

Anthony thrust again, opening her up until his balls rested against her ass and she let out a keening whine, eyes focused somewhere in the middle-distance above them. Every muscle in his body tensed as he drew back and plunged forward, fucking her without regard for the restraints tethering her to the frame of the bed. There was no give to those ropes, which made each of his thrusts punctuate in a deliciously hard stop.

Again and again.

She was either wet now, or bleeding, but it was inconsequential because it eased his movements. Her body tightened, gripped him, tried to force him out... and it felt good. Amplified his sensations, waking up his nerves with physical pleasure. This was the closest to human he ever felt. Reaching for an orgasm. Warm, soft flesh pinned beneath his hard body.

She just didn't appreciate it.

Slaves always became still at this point. Some sort of

primordial instinct in their brain taking over, reminding them that submission was the only option when a predator had them pinned. The same ancient force that demanded he fuck her just a little harder, not holding back, just to cement that knowledge in her mind.

Weak versus strong. Female versus male. There was only ever one victor.

Heat thawed his cold self-control as he moved inside her, reveling in the pained sounds slipping from her lips. Pleasure in all its chemical glory flooded his veins, fingers wrapping under her shoulders to dig into the delicate flesh that held such promise. In the coming days he would bring her such sweet agony, he would make her scream until her throat was raw, and then he'd fuck it just to remind her of her place.

This place.

Deep, hard thrusts sent tremors up his spine, making his bones as tight as her cunt felt. There was nothing quite like this, the delirious feeling of complete power over another human being. Next time he'd leave her arms free so she could try to scratch, to fight him off, and then he'd hold her down and destroy her just a little more. Prove to her that the ropes were merely convenience, not a deciding factor.

Even if she'd been free to run from him in the house, he would have caught her, hurt her, forced her to the ground so he could take what he wanted. Like this. Like property.

This was almost as sweet as her screams.

His pleasure in her pain. Slick cunt hot and clenching

tight. His mind was blurring, fuzzing — his orgasm close — but he wanted this to last just another few moments.

Capturing her chin, he forced her to look at him.

Pure desolation. Bleak, brown eyes met his as he thrust hard enough that his own hips felt the bruises he left. She was crying silently, fat tears rolling from the corners of her eyes into that California blonde hair that his customers had begged for.

Just a little more.

Take just a little more from her.

"You're never getting free," he whispered, their lips almost touching. Close enough to be lovers in some alternate universe. "Ever."

She squeezed him tight as a fist as her body contorted, the agonized cry in her voice better than any moan as he took her. Forcing himself deep just as the fire she'd kindled boiled over and left his balls in pulses that turned his vision white.

His hand had slipped to her throat as he'd come, gripping hard, and the desperate gape of her mouth was a lovely thing to see. Instead of letting her breathe, he settled himself between her hips, ensuring she felt the warmth seeping around his buried cock. "You're nothing but a set of holes, slave. Nod for me so I know you understand."

Chest jerking with her urge for oxygen, she finally bent her head in a perfunctory nod and he released her throat. The coughs as she tried to rip air back into her lungs made her body squeeze him inside her, a pleasant follow-up to his release. He reminded himself to enjoy it, to revel in every desperate, inarticulate sound leaving her lips. Wordless suffering that had nothing to do with his softening cock still buried deep. *That* pain was over and done with. *This?* This was all her. Her mind, her fear, her hope dying just a little further.

Tracing her lip with his thumb, he held her chin in place so she couldn't pull away. There was nothing quite as good as this fleeting moment, the moment they realized they were lost, and as he slid free and looked down between them he felt a smile move over his lips.

"It's okay, slut, you're supposed to bleed the first time."

FIVE

Beth

———————

The sound of the shower kicking on made Beth twitch against the sheets, opening her eyes just enough to confirm that he wasn't still standing by the bed.

He was gone.

Oh God…

Everything hurt. Wrists and ankles stung under the coarse rope. The lingering aches of the cattle prod pulsed — but none of it could match the dull, throbbing pain between her legs. At first it had been agonizingly sharp, a burning tear as he'd sawed his way inside her… and then it had faded. Or she had simply adjusted, numbed to it, detached as he'd used her.

If only she could ignore the warmth seeping from inside her. Block out the way the air cooled the wetness on her thighs, the drip of it moving down over her ass into the flat sheet on the bed.

Did I really bleed?

She was tempted to lift her head, to look and verify his claim, but she didn't want to know. In this case, ignorance truly was bliss. Unfortunately, there was no denying that he'd come inside her. He had been sure to make her feel that, even as he'd choked her, and now she could feel it leaking out of her.

A whimper clawed its way up her throat, escaping through clenched teeth, and she uselessly pulled at the ropes, waking up the stinging burns that confirmed she'd broken skin in her struggles. All she wanted was to curl up in a ball, close her eyes, and go to sleep. Forget about every word he'd spoken, every fucked-up rule he'd made her recite — but he wouldn't even allow her that. Still spread wide, vulnerable in her pain for the cameras that she could now see winking at the corners of the room. One shiny glass eye directly above, looking straight down at her. Staring into it, she wondered who was watching this.

What kind of person could watch this and enjoy it?

'The ones that he wants to sell you to.' Her mind's answer was spectacularly unhelpful, and she cursed aloud and internally as she tried to pull one hand, and then the other, through the ropes. Too tight, it was only making her hands hurt, her thumbs aching as she tried to squeeze them past the loops.

Useless.

It was all so useless, but she refused to give in. Refused to just fall into this sick game of his. *No.* She wouldn't be one of those women who succumbed to their captor like in Beauty and the Beast. Some version of Stockholm syndrome on fairy-tale boosted steroids. He wasn't a prince. There was nothing good in him. This asshole was nothing but violence and cold psychosis, and she wouldn't give him the satisfaction of bending her to his rules. He'd already shown her that giving in brought nothing but more pain, more torment. Maybe if she fought it hard enough, he'd even give up. Let her go.

Fool.

That was a slim chance. A stupid idea to even plant in her head… but if he really planned to bring others here, more people to do what he had done, wouldn't death be better?

Maybe… but someone might have seen her being taken. There could be people looking for her right now, police tracking down whatever car he'd used to bring her here. Her family would report her missing for sure. It was a shred of hope. She just had to be strong.

The sound of the shower cut off and her heartbeat filled the silence, pounding in her ears as she strained to listen to the movements of him in the bathroom. The quiet clap of the shower door, the subtle scrape of a towel over skin — so much to be heard when she held her breath in her lungs.

Her body jerked involuntarily as something dropped inside the bathroom. A clatter of noise that sent a fresh rush of adrenaline through her veins, making her lungs tight, her heart rate skyrocketing.

It was still a few more minutes before he appeared. Back in his suit, even his shining belt returned to his waist.

When had he picked up the jacket and belt?

His eyes moved over her without any sort of emotion. Ice blue, and she hated that on the outside he seemed attractive. Fine features, a tall and athletic frame. But there was nothing inside him. He was a wasteland, and he wanted to drag her down with him. Hollow her out just like him.

"I will release you if you promise not to be stupid." Even his voice was cold and empty. Unfeeling. There was no chance she could reach whatever dregs of humanity remained inside him — if there had ever been any at all.

"Okay," she muttered, but he only tilted his head.

"Did you forget the rules?" he asked.

I will never call you Master. The words threatened to leave her lips, a vehement anger suffusing every inch of her body, but she bit down. Stayed silent as she glared at him from the bed.

He moved closer, one casual step after another, as if the time meant nothing to him. "Would you like to take a shower?"

Yes. More than anything she wanted to stand under scalding water, to erase his touch from her skin, the texture of him between her thighs, but she wouldn't give in. Couldn't. If she gave him this, what more would he want? When would it ever stop? She knew without asking further questions that his plans for her were nothing less than total obedience. He wanted her to respond to his fucked-up list of rules, to follow them blindly.

Beth decided then that she would be a grave disappointment.

The man moved closer and she flinched as he leaned against the bed and ran his hand up the inside of her thigh. When two of his fingers slipped through the wet folds of her sex, she tensed, locked up — it was impossible to avoid her reaction. Pain spiked inside her. Definitely torn. Bleeding. She didn't even need his confirmation.

"Does it hurt?" he asked, the threat of a smile ticking up the corner of his mouth.

Sick fuck.

Biting down on her lip, she tried to stay silent, to swallow the whimpers, but when he forced a third finger inside her she cried out. Tears rolling, hands forming fists as her core spasmed, twitched around the invasion.

"You're going to be such a lovely broken doll. Someone will pay so much to make you cry like this." He thrust his fingers inside her already bruised and violated flesh. "To hurt you like this. Worse than this."

"*Worse?*" she asked, and immediately regretted it. She'd opened her eyes just in time to see his smile spread.

"Oh yes… this was just an introduction. I have so much more to show you." He slid his fingers from her and the tension fled her muscles as the pain dulled to a throb once more. "Open."

Beth shook her head, clenching her teeth as he brought his hand towards her mouth. The shine on his fingers made her cringe, whining low in her chest.

"You will learn…" He grabbed her face hard with his other hand, fingers digging into her jaw until he forced it open. Sliding tainted digits over her tongue, she tasted the mix of them, the linger of soap, the hint of copper and salt, just before she gagged as he pushed them too far. "Fighting me only results in punishment for you. Suffering."

He gagged her again, and her stomach threatened to heave, but he didn't even flinch as he pressed down on her tongue and forced her mouth wider with his knuckles.

"I will enjoy making you into a thing. Stripping everything from you that you think makes you a person." Another plunge of his fingers into her throat, wet choking sounds escaping as she tried to deny his words. The inevitability of them.

You won't win.

You won't.

"Suck, slut. Clean your mess off my fingers." He released her jaw, fingers still too far back on her tongue, and she immediately bit down.

His body jerked, but he was fast, responding instantly to her pathetic defiance. Fist buried in her hair as he wrenched her head back, fingers pulled free from her mouth, and then he backhanded her. Wet knuckles popping loudly against her cheek as pain starburst and spread across her face.

Why had she done that? Why, why, why…

"That was very stupid, cunt. Do you know how my customers would handle biting?" He shook her by her hair, somehow still calm, steady gaze burning into her eyes as she tried to fight the tears. "They'd knock each and every one of your pretty white teeth out. Is that what you want?"

"NO!" she shouted, and the fear took over. Sobbing as she twisted in the ropes, the stinging burn a chastisement.

"Beg."

Shaking, she swallowed the abundance of saliva pooling in

her mouth and pleaded. "I'm sorry I bit you, please don't —" Fear made her hiccup, whining as she clenched her eyes shut so she wouldn't have to look into his eyes. "Please not my teeth, I won't do it again. I'll never do it again. I swear!"

He released her hair and she heard him walking around the bed, opening her eyes to see him at a cabinet where he slid a drawer open. Closed it. All so calm, so fucking slowly. But the knife in his hand when he turned around made her sob harder. *Oh God.*

"No, no, no! I'm sorry! I said I was SORRY!"

Walking with that even, measured pace of his, he approached the end of the bed. The knife touched the arch of her foot and she stilled instantly, terrified and gasping, air wheezing in tightening lungs. "You're going to be so entertaining," he said softly, almost to himself, and then he raised his eyes to hers. "Don't move."

This time there was no urge to be defiant. He slid the sharp edge of the knife under the rope and worked at it until it broke, freeing her ankle. Raw, bright red skin revealed.

He repeated the action at her other ankle but, when she moved her leg, he caught it and snapped her back to the bed, the sharp edge of the knife against her calf. "I told you not to move, slave."

Beth found herself nodding, but a tiny voice inside her argued. Urged her to fight. To kick him. To hurt him.

She didn't do anything.

Lying as still as he'd commanded, she pressed her lips together and tried to slow her breathing, to stop the tears as he freed one wrist. His slow walk around the end of the bed made her flinch, because she was keeping her legs open for him, and she knew he was looking between them at the place he'd already hurt her.

This was just an introduction. I have so much more to show you.

As her last limb was cut free, he put a knee on the bed beside her arm, his weight making the bed sink. She flinched as he reached towards her — but then his hand slid under her neck and she heard the click of something metallic.

Why did she keep opening her eyes?

He was there above her, looking down like she was still just a bug pinned to a board for him. Only now the ropes were gone, and she wasn't moving by choice. She was obeying, and the camera in the ceiling was watching.

"Open your mouth."

There were a hundred pleas she wanted to say, a thousand questions she wanted to ask. So many *whys* and useless things. Instead, she opened her fucking mouth.

"Wider."

She stretched her lips, her aching jaw, and he brought the knife into view. For a nanosecond she started to close her mouth, but his head tilted the tiniest fraction and she stopped. Kept it open, eyes glued to the shining edge of the blade.

"I want to make something clear, so that you don't misunderstand." Turning the knife in his fingers, he angled it down and then slid the flat of it over her bottom lip, the sharp point inside her mouth. "I am not merciful. When you are disobedient, you will be punished. Severely."

A whimper escaped her throat, but as the flat of the blade moved deeper and brushed her tongue — she froze. Pressed her tongue to the floor of her mouth, tears making her eyes sting as the metal stroked back and forth.

"I will let you keep your teeth, but *only* because you are prettier with them than without them. Worth more." His other hand lifted, brushing hair off her forehead, unsticking it from the drying tears on her cheeks. "But at some point, I will fuck your throat, and I want you to remember this moment. Think about this knife as I slide my cock into your mouth, and remember that if you ever bite me again, I can do terrible things to you and still leave you pretty on the outside. Blink if you understand."

She blinked slowly, squeezing her eyes shut before she opened them again.

"Good girl." Withdrawing the knife with the careful, measured pace he seemed to do everything except fucking, she watched it until he held it above her. Only then did she gasp air into burning lungs, licking her lips, too terrified to move. "Now that you understand, it's time for your punishment."

SIX

Anthony

Scrolling through her medical file on his phone, Anthony stood next to the cart as other shoppers moved past him. Some glared at him, one woman looked him over, but it was all white noise. The haze of humans existing, the metallic clatter of carts, the beeping of registers. So much white noise. It made it somewhat difficult to focus on the small device in his hands, but then he found what he was looking for.

Memorizing the brand of birth control, he verified that it was monophasic, and then sent the order in. Computers were so much easier than people. Just zeros and ones, and once you understood them you could make them do whatever you wanted. No need to threaten them or slide a knife into their proverbial mouths. They just worked. Every time.

Tucking his phone into his pocket he walked down the aisle, adding items to his cart from the list in his mind. Food for him, and food for her. She wouldn't actually *need* to eat for a while, but hunger was an excellent motivator. Still, when he fed her, it would not be from his plate.

That was Marcus' fetish.

Of course, Marcus had the culinary palate of a street dog. He would eat well when he thought about it, but he'd also seen his brother eat a package of beef jerky with the same satisfaction as filet mignon with béarnaise sauce.

His phone buzzed repeatedly in his pocket and he answered without looking at the screen. Only one person had this number. "Yes?"

"You started with the cattle prod?" Marcus didn't even bother with a hello, knowing it was pointless, but his tone was still challenging to dissect. Without other cues to help him along, Anthony couldn't tell if the intent of the question was positive or negative. Delight or disgust. Yet another reason he avoided the phone.

"I did," he confirmed needlessly. Clearly, his brother had been watching the recording of the live stream and already knew the answer.

"You haven't even had her a whole day."

Glancing at his watch, he noted it had only been about fourteen hours. "Correct."

"You should've let me have her first, this is going to make her more challenging." A growl and a curse punctuated his statement.

Definitely a negative response.

"How will it be more challenging? Enlighten me." Coddling Marcus was an exhausting exercise, but one that was required to keep him engaged and productive. Without the opportunity to vent his silly frustrations, his brother's work quality plummeted. He could sulk like a child for days.

"You started out too strong. All pain, no pleasure. What incentive does she have to respond to you now?"

"Avoiding it," he clipped, looking around at the milling cattle with their rickety carts creating so much noise that it was unlikely anyone could even hear him. Regardless, it was always wise to be cautious.

"Did she even come when you fucked her?"

"No, but that is where you always make your mistakes. It is not about them, they are nothing." Anthony sighed when Marcus muttered on the other end of the phone. Worse than having to listen to him speak was having to listen to him when he was incoherent.

At least when the slaves were incoherent, they were usually making pleasant sounds.

"She bled."

"Yes, I've already received several emails asking me to do it again, and in other ways." Anthony wondered if she would scream as he took her ass. There was a good chance no one had ever fucked her there — such a treat to be the first.

"We don't make them bleed," Marcus stated it like there was some book of rules to which they were *both* held. As if every rule he made Marcus follow was not written by his own hand.

Even the rules on the wall were his.

Everything was, but Marcus forgot that sometimes.

"Sometimes we do. You have become overzealous in the past and done the same."

"Is that what you were? *Overzealous?*" His brother tried to mock his tone, mimic him, but there was too much emotion in Marcus to ever succeed in that.

"That is ridiculous, and you know it. Did you want to have a conversation or were you simply calling to replay the events of last night for me?" Bored already with Marcus' antics, Anthony smiled when he saw the artisan cheese counter was open. At least there was one benefit to shopping on a Saturday morning when people crowded the store.

"I want to talk to you about not fucking up this slave! This is why it takes you almost three fucking months to get anywhere with—" Marcus continued to rant as Anthony held the phone down to his side and approached the counter.

"Hello, sir. Are you interested in trying one of our aged Goudas?" The smiling woman was wearing a black apron, her auburn hair pulled into a high ponytail at the back of her head. Her nametag read: *Amanda.*

"Yes. Where is it from?" Anthony watched as the woman looked him over with a quick glance before cutting off a slice from the wedge of cheese in front of her.

"Beemster, it's a Dutch brand. Quite good, aged eighteen months, and it has a sweet finish." Amanda rattled off her knowledge before handing him the tiny slice on a petite napkin.

"Thank you, just a moment." Lifting the phone back to his

ear, he could hear Marcus muttering curses and insults. "Are you done, Marcus?"

"Where the fuck did you go? Are you at the fucking grocery store?" He was angry, *that* was an easy emotion to identify but, before he answered, he leaned the cell phone against his shoulder so he could break off a bite of the cheese. It was as delightful as the woman had described.

"This is good," he acknowledged, and the woman beamed.

"Are you ignoring me, Anthony? What the fuck! Did you leave the girl already?" His shouting was loud enough that Amanda's eyebrows pulled together slightly, her eyes flicking to the cell phone.

"I'm here, and yes, I needed to get groceries, so I am at the grocery store. Currently, I'm sampling an aged gouda from Beemster, it—"

"I don't give a FUCK about cheese, Anthony!" Marcus interrupted him, shouting, and Anthony simply sighed as he savored the last bite.

"That is quite clear. One moment." Holding the phone away from his ear, he turned his attention back to the woman in front of him. "My brother is emotional. I apologize for the interruption. What other cheeses would you recommend?"

"Oh!" For a moment she was flustered, a delicate blush of color coming to her cheeks, and then she leaned down and opened the sliding back of the case. An instant later she lifted out a Comté that he already knew he enjoyed. "This is a French cheese called Comté from Saint Antoine. If you like Gruyère, then I'm sure you'll enjoy this, it's one of my absolute favorites. They actually skim it and heat it in copper vats, and when it's aged it just takes on the *best* flavor, and I really think you'll like it if you try it. I mean, if you like cheese."

The woman was babbling, nervous. He could tell by the slight shaking of her hands as she unwrapped the cellophane from around the wedge. Her knowledge of the cheese was impressive, even more so that she knew the process of making it.

Why on earth was she wasting her skills standing under the abysmal lighting of this grocery store? She should be at an artisan shop directing people who would appreciate it.

"It sounds delightful," Anthony replied when she stared at him, her blush now a bright pink across her nose and cheeks. It brought out the red in her hair. She handed over a fresh napkin and he took it as he placed the phone back to his ear.

"—asshole. There's a fucking slave waiting, and this bitch is talking about cheese."

"Language, Marcus," he chastised, feeling a frisson of irritation as his brother insulted her. "I'm shopping, she is answering my questions. If you're done losing your temper, we can hang up."

"Where the fuck is the girl, Anthony?"

A smile curled his mouth as he bit down on the Comté and the quiet nuttiness of brown butter coated his tongue. If Marcus was asking *that* question, it meant he had not continued to watch the feed. "Why don't you check the video?"

Pulling the phone away, he nodded at her, crumpling the empty napkin in his fist. "I'll take some of the Beemster, the Comté, and one other that you recommend."

"What would you like?" she asked, so eager to serve.

"Surprise me." His response made her bounce on her toes, a broad smile on her face as she crouched behind the counter to seek out something that could *surprise* him. As if that were possible... but at least it would be something delicious. The girl had a good palate.

Looking down at his phone, he moved out of the call and brought up the control panel for the video controls in the house. Keeping the phone close to his chest, he looked down at her pale form against the concrete. It was shiny from the thin layer of water he'd left her in after her wake-up call, her collar chained to the floor with less than two feet of lead. Not enough for her to sit up all the way, which he had done on purpose.

Knowing that by now Marcus was looking at the video, he tapped the remote activation button and watched her scream, body jerking, water splashing. Then he turned off the electric jolt and moved back to the phone screen so he could rest it against his shoulder. "Do you see?" he asked Marcus.

"She's going to get sick, and you're not even there if something went wrong. What if she'd reacted badly to the shock?"

"Are you questioning me, Marcus?" The edge to his tone had made the smile fade from Amanda's face, and he sighed, offering what he hoped would pass for an authentic, human smile. "What did you choose for the third one?"

"Um…" Her blue eyes flicked to the phone in his hand, and then, as if she remembered her customer service training, she plastered the smile back on her face. "I, um, I hope you like it. It's more subtle, but very good. A Pyrénées Sheep cheese from Abbaye de Belloc. We only just got some this month, so I really hope more people buy some so they keep it in stock."

"Well, if I enjoy it, I'll make sure to come back and buy more."

"If you like *her* so much, why not just fucking take her? She can talk to you about cheese while you electrocute her," Marcus muttered.

"No," he replied, abrupt, and then he took the packages from Amanda, watching her reaction as her fingers touched his. The flush was back, and he wondered if she was aroused or afraid of him.

Human emotions were so needlessly complicated.

"I really do hope you like them."

"Thank you, Amanda." He set the cheeses in the basket and then pushed the cart away, pressing the phone to his ear.

"*Amanda.*" Marcus huffed. "Maybe I'll take her and bring her up here. See what she can teach me about cheese while I—"

"The answer is no."

"What the fuck, Anthony? Are you really protecting that cunt?" He laughed. "She sounded young, was she pretty? Is that the deal, you want her for yourself after you're done with Beth?"

"I *want* her to be here so that this hovel of a store continues to carry decent cheeses. If you do something without my permission, there will be consequences." He kept his voice hushed as he paused near the bagged lettuce, but his brother knew he did not make idle threats and Marcus' laughter wound down to a growl.

"Don't talk to me like I'm one of the slaves."

"Then don't act out like one." Anthony got in line, ready to be out of the presence of so many squalling children and chattering people. "Have you made progress on your house?"

"I just woke up an hour ago."

"Well, then perhaps you should get to work instead of interfering with mine. I was doing this before you were even aware."

"I *know*, asshole. You don't have to keep pointing it out. I think I've more than proven I've got my own set of skills," Marcus mumbled under his breath, and Anthony decided he was done with this coddling session.

"We'll see how you handle this new enterprise before we make any real judgments on your skills."

"You're just afraid I'm better at this than you!" Marcus was angry. Throwing a temper tantrum like he had when they were children and he'd lost an unknown number of games of checkers.

All emotion, no strategy.

"We will see," was Anthony's only reply before he ended the call. Stacking the various items on the automatic belt, he reminded himself to stop at the pharmacy to get the girl's pills, and then he would return to see if her attitude had improved.

SEVEN

Beth

Her teeth were chattering and, even curled into a ball on the floor, Beth couldn't manage to concentrate her body heat enough to stop shivering. The thin layer of water atop the concrete seemed to sap the warmth from the air as well as her skin, and just the existence of this horrible room confirmed how screwed she was.

Normal people didn't have rooms set several inches into the floor so water could pool half an inch deep. They didn't have hoses installed inside, or steel brackets embedded in the floor for chaining girls by leather collars. Collars locked closed with a tiny version of the padlock that kept the chain fixed in place.

Another set of shivers shook her, making her curl up tighter, as far away from the bracket in the floor as the chain allowed. It didn't make it easier. Beth still couldn't believe she was in this place. This room. This house. Couldn't understand what she'd done wrong, what misstep she'd made that had brought her to him. She couldn't even remember him taking her. There was a hole in her memory even after the drugs had completely left her system.

She remembered leaving work, walking down the same sidewalk she always did. Heading towards the public lot they shared with several other companies, and then — *nothing*. Absolutely nothing until she'd woken up on that bed.

But at least the bed had been soft, and warmer than this nightmare room.

Trying to sleep on concrete all night had been almost impossible, and she was sure it was only the physical exhaustion, her body wrung out by pain and fear, that had eventually made her pass out.

And then the motherfucker had woken her up with the fucking hose. Cold water blasting her at full pressure.

Are you ready to be obedient, he'd asked. Stoic, standing several feet away so the spray bouncing off her skin wouldn't reach him.

Beth had told him to go to hell, and he had left, leaving the hose running on the floor to slowly fill the room. An icy puddle turned into a pool, spreading, eventually touching her skin no matter how she skittered back from it. Inching its way across the concrete until it had crept into every corner.

She had no idea how long he was gone, but he returned in a clean button down and slacks, which did *not* match the tall rubber boots on his feet. When he'd finally turned off the water, she'd already been cold, but that wasn't the worst part of this nightmare room.

It was the electric shock that moved through the water whenever he touched something on his phone.

Blinding pain, the air ripped from her lungs on a scream, unable to draw another breath until he stopped it. She'd earned two more shocks in those first hours. One for telling him to go fuck himself, and the second for staying silent when he'd told her to recite the rules.

Whining, freezing, sore — he had towered over her, breathing evenly while she panted, and the chaos tore cohesive thoughts to shreds.

You should think over your decisions, slave. His last words before he'd walked out. Left her in this fucking concrete room, with the A/C running, soaking wet and unable to even push up onto all fours because the chain was too fucking short.

Was this really her future?

The idea was almost too horrible to process, but once it had appeared in her head it wouldn't be quiet. It coiled in the center of her mind, a dangerous viper with icy blades for fangs, hissing, waiting. Waiting for her to accept this nightmare as reality. *Her* reality.

She didn't want to accept anything. Beth wanted to rage, to rip the chain from the floor — not like she hadn't tried — but it was all so useless. The man was so much stronger than her, and colder than the water pooled around her.

It had been ridiculously easy for him to push her through the house with his fingers wrapped around the back of the collar. Pulling it flush to her throat, tightening it as she prepared for his promised punishment. With the metal of the knife still fresh on her tongue, Beth hadn't even tried to fight. She had let him haul her into this room. Let him push her to her knees. Watched like a sacrificial lamb as he'd gathered chain from a metal table and tethered her to the bracket embedded in the concrete.

She had expected violence. Expected him to hit her, or at the very least to shout at her —but he'd done nothing.

Turning around in his polished shoes he had simply walked out of the room, the heavy door shutting with a loud *clap*, and she'd been alone. The concrete had bruised her limbs, made her hips ache, and she'd *thought* she felt cold. But last night was nothing compared to this.

Her bones ached, each shiver making them jerk against stiff muscles and tendons, and she almost laughed at the bitter idea that cold was used to make pain *stop*. Cold hurt worse than any volleyball injury in high school or college, hurt worse than the time she'd been rear-ended at a stoplight — it was nothing but hurt. Pinpricks of fire as her nerves sparked in desperation, and then the deep, shuddering ache that followed every bout of shivers. The foolish, automatic response of her body trying to keep her alive.

It would be wiser to die before he came back.

Beth sniffled, curled tighter as the thought burrowed close to the viper that promised a future more hellish than even this. Torture, rape… or death.

Are those really my only options?

Being rescued, the idea of police bursting in to help her, that seemed far away. Too impossible to hope for. The warm tracks of tears across the bridge of her nose were the only way she realized she was crying, too cold to make noise, too distracted by the weak shudders of her body to focus on her hitched breaths.

None of it mattered a second later when the *pop* of the electric current turning on reminded her of just how much pain she could be in. A scream tried to escape her lips just before her head cracked against the concrete floor, vision turning white as every inch of her body went rigid, agony coursing along her nerves like they were open wounds. Salted and burning. It felt like it lasted forever, lungs trapped around too little air, and then the buzzing ended and she went limp. Water lolling back and forth around her, tiny waves on the ocean of her ruin.

As her eyes regained focus, flickering on and off like a cheap movie reel, she saw him.

Standing over her, head tilted to the side, upside down from her point of view. Dark hair cut so that it laid perfectly, not a strand out of place, and those cold blue eyes that held no human emotion to speak of — he was simply watching her. Gaze drifting down her body as she tried to pull air back into her lungs, too weak to even try and shield her nakedness.

Not like any of it mattered.

He'd seen everything.

And he didn't even seem interested. It wasn't lust she saw in his face, it wasn't hate, or rage, or hunger, or joy — it was nothing. An absolute emptiness behind a face that could have been attractive on someone with a soul.

His silence grated like sandpaper on her frayed nerves, the cold returning as her body abandoned the memory of the shock and let the icy water creep back into her perception.

A shiver shook her again, teeth clattering loudly in the quiet, broken again by the soft splash of the water as she managed to bend one leg against the other to try and block the view between her thighs.

There were five cameras.

One at the center of each wall, and a final straight above the bracket in the floor.

Whatever assholes sat on the other side of those glass eyes had seen everything as well, but she didn't have to gift it to them. Not if she could avoid it.

The man hadn't moved, had barely breathed from what she could tell. An automaton. A shell of a person in fine clothes. "What do you want from me?" she croaked, voice cracking.

Weak. So weak.

"Everything," he answered, taking a step, and then another, until he stood beside her hip and she could see him clearly. Still in his big rubber boots, his protection from the electric current he tormented her with. "We've already had that discussion. Now is when you decide if you'd like to start being obedient."

It was so tempting to curse him, to damn him again. To rage against everything he'd already done to her — but it was the threat of what he *would* do that kept her silent.

"Well?" he asked.

"I'm cold," she whispered. A shiver coming on cue, her aching joints tightening to make her whimper.

"I know." His gaze slid over her body again. "Would you like to get up? Leave this room?"

Something dangerous lurked behind the offer, something with teeth, but she couldn't resist. "Yes."

That strange smile graced his features again. "Then tell me the rules, slave."

Even her reaction to that word was dulled, slowed by the cold, the pain, the memory of the knife in her mouth. "Don't bite."

A strange huff left him, what might have been a laugh had he been a real person. "That is *not* one of the rules, but I am encouraged to know you retained that lesson. Now… recite the rules."

Bastard.

Beth wanted to scream at him again. To shout like she had that morning, but her fingers were stiff and almost useless in the cold. Even the stinging burns from the rope had faded from her awareness, and that was concerning.

Turning her head, eyes focusing on the inflamed, broken skin at her wrist, she knew it should hurt more than it did — but nothing was getting through the cold. She needed out of this room.

"I am not a person." Everything was empty as the words moved past her numb lips, but she continued in a daze, struggling to remember his poster of fucked-up expectations. "I should address you as Master."

Never, she promised herself. Holding onto that one flapping scrap of her dignity.

"Continue." He walked away from her towards a panel on the wall, pressing buttons before it popped open.

"I have to crawl. Ask permission for everything."

"For what *specifically?*" he asked, shifting something inside the panel just before a click came from the far side of the bracket in the floor. The sound of water rushing into pipes made hope flicker inside her. Dim and desperate.

I just want to be warm.

"Slave?" The man was looking at her, his hand still inside the panel, and she dropped her head back to the floor so she didn't have to see his dead eyes.

"Permission to orgasm"—*never going to happen*—"to speak to you. And I cannot wear clothes."

Air sucked loudly into the pipe, the swirl of the water down the drain visible as she turned her head to the side. Shivers rushed through her again, tightening her weak, exhausted muscles once more.

So tired.

She was so tired.

Would it be so terrible to die?

"There are worse things than the cold, slut. You're not done." He leaned against the wall by the panel, watching as she turned onto her side.

Beth answered the thinning water instead of him. "I must keep my eyes down. Thank you when you hurt me."

"*Punish,*" he corrected.

"Right." She did not repeat the correction, racking her brain for the list, but there was nothing more in her head. Nothing but the horrible memories of everything he'd already done to her, the nagging ache between her thighs as she clenched her internal muscles.

"You forgot that you must kneel in all rooms, and again whenever I return."

"I can't kneel." Moving her feeble grip to the chain, she tugged it so that it clattered against the metal in the floor.

"I am aware. I didn't want you able to kneel, I wanted you on the floor." His footsteps slapped wet and heavy against the concrete as he approached her once more, but she didn't turn her eyes to him. Not even when she could see the towering form of him in her peripheral vision. "Do you understand that this is where you belong?"

"No." The word was out before her blurry mind could think to stop her, and she just closed her eyes, waiting for pain. Another shock.

Instead, he simply crouched down and used a key to open the padlock that held the chain to the floor. Wrapping his fist around the metal links, he stood, dragging her up by force, her body rebelling against the movement. Joints screaming, muscles revolting. Reminding her in fits and starts of the chill, the lingering aches from the electricity and so many hours on the concrete.

Beth found herself sitting up, legs curled at her side, one hand braced in a puddle left behind from the water draining down the dark hole at the center of the room. The man tugged the chain higher, forcing her head to angle back, but she aimed her gaze just to the left of his head.

"Look at me." It was a command, not a request. Clipped, abrupt, hard as ice.

She obeyed and hated herself for it.

"Tell me *thank you* and I'll let you take a warm shower."

Anthony

The girl was freezing, almost no color to her skin except for the darker tone of her areolas, and the hint of blue at her lips and fingernails. Her toes were hinting towards blue as well, and he knew what she needed to stay healthy. Alive.

Whether she got warm from him fucking her in a bed, or taking a shower alone, was up to her.

It had only been a couple of hours in the cold, but it had done exactly what he'd planned. Stripped her of another layer of that willpower she was clinging to so desperately. He could sense the struggle in her, recognizing it from the other girls he'd taken, broken. But this one was more of a challenge, which meant he could, and would, do *so much more* to her before she grew boring and docile.

Shifting his hand, he wrapped the chain around his hand another time, clenching his fist over the links to pull her higher, watching as she struggled to pull her legs beneath her so the strain on the collar wasn't so severe.

Oh, the things he would make her do to avoid the pain.

"Last chance, slut."

"*Thank you,*" she whispered, eyes down, but he tugged the chain instead of acknowledging her acquiescence.

"Louder."

"Thank you." Only a little louder, more of a growl, a promise of further defiance. Further opportunity to make her scream, and cry, and beg for a mercy that would never come.

It was that thought that made him smile again. He didn't wait for her to recognize his movement, he simply walked towards the door with the chain clamped tight in his grip. Her knees scraped over the damp concrete, scuttling after him with stiff limbs. She whimpered when he hauled her over the doorway, something impacting the lip of the room as she tried to stand, but he tugged the chain to keep her in her proper place.

On her knees.

Scrambling to keep up with his pace.

He returned to the bedroom she'd awoken in, tapping the code into the lock as he hid the pad with his body. Not that she was coherent enough yet to pay attention.

Her shuddering breaths, interspersed with whimpers, were music to his ears. Or it *would* be music to his ears if he could enjoy music at all. Screams and cries were his music, and he would make her a symphony before he sold her.

Tugging the chain hard, he hauled her inside and then buckled her to the floor. Releasing the metal links, he ignored her whimpers to shut the door behind them. It auto-locked, as it always did, and he waited as she caught her breath. One hand braced on the floor between her knees as she pushed herself upright, forming into an almost perfect presentation.

A happy accident, he was sure, but still delightful for the customers on the cameras.

She had potential. So much potential. He just needed to carve away everything else until all that was left was the broken slave at the core of who she thought she was. Take away the sense of self, the sense of worth, the concept of individuality — *then* she'd be ready to sell.

The girl's brown eyes lifted, met his, and he contemplated slapping her. But she self-corrected too quickly, gaze diverting to the hardwoods under her naked, shivering limbs. It was likely she wasn't even aware of the way her flesh trembled, it had probably been so steady for the last hour or so that she could only feel the more violent tremors.

Her body's desperate attempt to create warmth.

"Slave." It was only a word for now, but he noted how her head lifted slightly. *Almost* answering to it. Another step forward. "Ask for permission to have your shower."

It was the sudden tensing of her shoulders that telegraphed her resistance this time. No eye contact, no foul-mouthed curses, no violent thrashing. The tension bled out of her with the next hard shiver of her body, and he could hear her teeth chattering as she tried to stymie it. "May I please shower?"

"Finish your request properly," Anthony commanded and watched her body still, only the subtle tremors making her muscles jump unconsciously, but the girl stayed quiet. Sighing, he threaded his fingers into her damp hair and tightened, ripping her upright so that she had no choice but to shuffle on her knees and shins as he half-dragged her into the bathroom. The light switch instantly brightened the room, and he knew the action had activated the cameras so that his customers could enjoy this.

He wanted to make her scream for defying him, but that would have to wait. Her core temperature needed to elevate first, then he could torment her again.

There is plenty of time. Patience is necessary.

Dropping her onto the tiled floor, he opened the standing shower and turned the water on mid-way so it could start to warm. The girl had said something, but it had been impossible to hear over the sound of the shower. "Did you want to speak, slave?"

"I'm sorry," she repeated meekly. It was astonishing how small she looked against the dark, slate tiles of the bathroom. This would be a good place to fuck her. Fresh from a bath, shaved smooth, her lithe limbs spread against the dull gray of the floor. Her cries would echo in this room, the customers would appreciate the contrast of her lighter skin to the slate, and each of his thrusts would be felt to their full extent. No give of a mattress beneath her ass.

Her ass.

Perhaps this could be where he fucked her there. Pinned to the cool floor, cheek against the tile — her sobs of pain would be guttural and perfect.

So many plans. So many ways to make her obedient and docile.

But first... reaching into the stream, he turned down the temperature a little until it was lukewarm, and then he fisted her hair again and yanked her to her feet. Her legs almost gave out, weak, her feet were probably numb — but that was her consequence for biting him. This was all a lesson that would settle deep into her brain.

Obey. Avoid pain.

Such a simple concept... but it took them so long to learn.

"Get in. Do not adjust the temperature of the water or I'll put you back in the punishment room." He nudged her forward and she braced her hands against the glass frame of the shower, gently stepping under the stream. A hiss of air slipped through her teeth, the lukewarm water probably felt boiling on her chilled skin, but, again, it was not his concern.

Shutting the shower door, he stepped back and leaned against the bathroom counter. Hands in his pockets, ignoring the hard outline of his cock, he watched as she simply stood under the water for a while.

Thawing. Skin flushing red as her blood warmed.

It wouldn't be the last time she earned that punishment. The second time she'd be more afraid, less recalcitrant. If she earned it a third time? He almost smiled. That was one of the places he'd broken so many girls. Just water and leather and chain. A little electric jolt now and then. Such simple things. Such simple pains. To be naked, and cold, and vulnerable.

Watching her running her hands over her body, her back to him, the round of her ass catching the lights from above, he knew she'd be back there soon. Knew he'd be able to sate the growing erection in his pants even sooner.

Maybe this time he'd let her fight.

EIGHT

Anthony

_____

"It's been five days, I'm coming back," Marcus growled into the phone, much too loudly, and Anthony flipped another page in the cookbook.

"Your presence is not necessary." Reaching for an egg, he cracked it against the edge of the bowl and let the insides spill out onto the mixture of seasonings he'd carefully measured.

"Are you kidding? You've been torturing her for almost a week, and she hasn't shown even the smallest hint of submitting."

His brother's tone held no hint of laughter, so Marcus already knew that he was not _kidding_. The eggshell went into the trash and he wiped his hands off on a towel before he took the fork from the counter and began to mix the coating according to the directions. Folding, not whisking.

"Anthony!"

"Yes?" He kept his tone steady as he worked the mixture to the right consistency.

"What the fuck are you doing?"

"Cooking. It's almost time for dinner." Setting the bowl down, he picked up the chicken breast and dredged it through the mixture, laying it out on the pan where it instantly sizzled in the heated olive oil. *Perfect.* Exactly as the recipe described. He liked it when things worked as designed.

"Are you feeding her?"

"Of course."

"How much?"

"Enough," he answered, already bored with the conversation.

"Tonight?"

"She had a can of soup yesterday."

"That's not enough and you know it. You're going to make her useless." A sound followed the other man's words that Anthony could only attribute to frustration, or disgust, or some other mercurial emotion that flitted through his little brother's mind.

"I assure you she is still quite usable." Parting the oven door enough to glance in at the couscous and Abbaye de Belloc stuffed tomatoes, he shut it quickly so that too much heat did not disperse. "I fucked her just this morning."

"*Right.*" Marcus laughed; a low chuckle that did not sound sincere. "And she didn't come, did she?"

"Your obsession with—"

"Of course, she didn't. The customers want to know they're capable of responding! You have to at least demonstrate it, and she'd fucking behave if she knew there were alternatives to your *games*."

Another gruff sound came over the line as Anthony used a spatula to shift the chicken in the pan so it wouldn't stick.

"I'm driving down tonight."

"No. You have incessantly pestered me with your ideas on running two *separate* operations for the past few months, and now that you are finally setting up your house you are focusing on this slut. Would you care to explain why?" He was prodding his brother's temper, one of his few entertainments in the world outside of food and breaking slaves, and at the next growl of rage from the phone he smiled.

It had worked. *Of course.*

Anthony flipped the chicken in the pan just as Marcus exploded on the other end of the line. "I'm *focusing* because you're fucking this up! The house is on schedule, but I've been watching the feed, and you've made absolutely zero progress." Another growl peppered the line. "Look, I have people installing the security measures on the doors right fucking now, and soon the house will be ready to go, but I need to be out of the way for them to finish replacing the floors and sealing over the windows. I'll be there before midnight."

"Her willpower will not last forever, Marcus. It's already flagging. She never attempts to stand in my presence unless I order her to, she keeps her eyes down, she crawls. She is adjusting to her new state as they all do." The timer on the microwave interrupted his update, and he pressed the little button to stop the incessant beeping.

"Yeah, *adjusting*. You've got her suspended in ropes again, how the fuck is she supposed to display submission when she's not even touching the floor?"

Anthony glanced at the feed on the tablet he had leaned against the backsplash. Pretty, pale limbs wound in perfectly clean lines of dark rope. "She looks submissive to me."

"She still hasn't called you Master."

With annoying precision, Marcus zeroed in on the issue that had actually managed to burrow its way into his thoughts. No matter what he'd done to the girl, she had yet to actually use the word as a title. He had forced her to say it in reference to the rules numerous times, but she refused to use it with him. Refused to acknowledge her position, even when that position was bound painfully off the floor.

It was a problem.

"I can get her to call me Master. I always do." Pride tainted Marcus' voice, and it was the one emotion that Anthony picked up on easily. His brother had always tried to best him, to exceed him in a variety of invented competitions — and he had consistently failed. Yet… this was an avenue where he might actually succeed. The slaves always clung to him, to his pathetic urge to give them pleasure. It wasn't subservience that he plucked from them; it was a need for companionship. The human need to connect, to want, to *feel*.

Anthony was only interested in the girl's fear, her slow dismantling — not her dedication or affection.

"Marcus, you just want to make her care for you like you have the others. *That* does not serve our purposes." Plucking the tray of tomatoes from the oven, he rested them on the cool side of the stovetop. "And, again, I will remind you that your presence is not requested or needed. She will break. It has only been a week."

"A week of nothing but her fighting you," Marcus retorted, defensive.

"It has been entertaining," he acknowledged, monitoring the chicken for the right moment to pull it from the searing heat.

"I doubt our customers feel the same way."

"Actually, I've received a flurry of emails asking me to punish her in various ways for her disobedience. They are ecstatically waiting for the moment I take her ass." Plunging the spatula beneath the chicken, Anthony lifted it and transferred it to a plate, immediately draping it in foil that crinkled loudly in the silence of the house.

"Why *have* you waited for that? You could have—"

"It's her last virginity, Marcus. Rushing it would only remove an opportunity to break her at the right moment." Anthony turned off the stove and oven, waiting for his dinner to be ready to eat. "When I claim it, she will have nothing left. Nothing hidden from me, or any of our customers. It will lay her bare and force her to recognize her situation. Wasting an opportunity like that is foolish."

"I could break her without fucking her ass."

He almost laughed at his brother's bravado, but he knew laughing would push him too far… so he held it back. Not exactly a challenge since his laughter was supposedly never *right*, even when he was sincerely entertained by Marcus' ridiculous bluster.

There were other ways to leverage the particular proclivities that his only sibling possessed. Perhaps the girl would respond to him, but Anthony had watched her maintain her stubbornness through agony and he held no concerns that a series of forced orgasms would cripple her defenses.

"You think you can break her? Get her to call you Master?" He dangled the temptation before his brother's ego and smiled as Marcus took the bait.

"Of course! That's what I've been telling you—"

"Then we will see if that's true when you arrive. Let's make a wager of it."

"Fuck off," Marcus growled. "I don't want—"

"If you don't think you can make her submit, then you may as well stay up there and monitor your house." Anthony glanced at the time on the microwave, calculating how long the chicken had been resting, and then he moved to the pantry to pluck another can of soup from the shelf.

Tomato. *How fitting*. He was having tomatoes this evening as well.

"What kind of wager?" Marcus asked, and he reveled in the moment where the hook caught, and his brother became just another one of his toys. Almost thirty years together and the man still hadn't learned.

"Oh, nothing much…" He poured the tomato soup into a pot, heating it atop the stove, occasionally stirring it as he outlined the details of the bet. Before he was even done, he knew Marcus would accept.

He always did.

His failure would be almost as entertaining as the girl's desolation if she managed to orgasm. Another crack in her willpower, something new for him to leverage as he spoke with her — it would almost make things *easier* if Marcus managed to give her pleasure. A new level of torment, a new low for her.

But she would never use the title with him. It would take so much more pain for the girl to say Master and mean it.

"You're serious?" Marcus asked, his interest clear.

"Of course. Do you accept the terms?" Anthony poured the soup out of the pot, directly into a wide bowl. On a whim, he went to the pantry and returned with oyster crackers, adding a small handful of them to the tray where her meal cooled. A gift.

"Fine. Yes. I accept, and I'm about to leave. I'll be there tonight."

"All right." Smiling, Anthony lifted the foil on his chicken and sighed. He'd need to take her down from the ropes, and watch her eat, which would take time. Tucking the tray of stuffed tomatoes and the pan of chicken into the still warm oven, he turned the heat on low. "Where would you like her?"

"The bedroom."

"Of course," he acknowledged, expecting nothing less from him.

"Don't do anything else to her before I get there." Was that nervousness in Marcus' tone? Anger? Either one was equally entertaining. He was already second-guessing his decision.

Too late.

"I will take her down from the ropes, feed her, and put her to bed. Then we will see what you can do with her."

"Good. I'm on my way," Marcus snapped. The sounds of him moving things on the other end of the line were loud, irritating.

"Then I shall see you soon." Ending the call, Anthony glanced at the tray of food and decided that a sugar spike would make things all the more entertaining. Pouring juice into a glass, he arranged it and glanced at her twitching form in the ropes again.

The time she'd spent suspended in bondage would leave her sore, but not too damaged. She would be confused by his actions in taking her down without further punishment, even more thrown off by the food and drink. Settling her into the soft bed without fucking her was going to set the girl on edge.

She would be waiting for something violent, something terrible. A fresh torture.

And then Marcus would arrive to use her.

It was perfect.

NINE

Beth

Beth hated the concrete room. Despised it. He called it *the punishment room*, but that wasn't it. The shit he was doing to her wasn't punishment, it was torture. From the first night he'd put her in there, she'd known it was a room meant for terrible things, but the cold, the water, the chain, and the fucking shocks were only the beginning.

She had seen the metal fixtures on the walls and ceiling that night, but she'd refused to dwell on them. Now, she knew first-hand what many of them were for.

The ones in the ceiling let him attach hooks that he could loop rope onto, winding it over her limbs in intricate patterns until she was finally lifted completely off the floor. Held up like an insect in a painful web where bulging knots dug into delicate flesh, where muscles cramped, where the cold sank deep with no opportunity to escape from it. To escape from *him*. More a spider than a person.

It was an apt description.

Today was the second time he'd strung her up like that,

and today she hadn't fought him. All he'd had to do was show her the little zapping baton and she had knelt gracelessly on the cold concrete, eyes down.

What are you supposed to call me?

His voice was inside her. Echoing in her thoughts like ghosts wandering an empty house, and she wanted him out. Exorcised. Wanted to be free of him, but just when she would manage to focus on something else — a song, a story, a memory — he would appear. Like he could feel when she was escaping from his influence. He would hurt her, rape her, and then speak to her in that infuriatingly calm tone.

What do you say, slave?

Everything was inverted. How many times had she said 'thank you' for the things he'd done to her? How many times had he demanded she finish the gratitude *properly*? And then how many times had he hurt her again to punish her?

No. It was torture. Not punishment.

This was as much psychological as it was physical. Beth still had enough sense of reality to know that. Even when her world had narrowed to the concrete room, the empty hallway, and the pretty bedroom with all its own horrors… she knew what he was doing. Trying to condition her to follow his ridiculous poster of rules.

She wouldn't follow them. At least, not *all* of them.

She was still a person. Still real.

But two things had become clear in her time with him. The bedroom was his version of a reward — a soft bed, sheets, a bathroom. The concrete one was punishment — cold, discomfort, and only a drain when she needed to relieve herself.

But in both rooms, he hurt her.

He had taken her against the concrete floor just as viciously as he'd taken her in the bed on the first night. Had chained her to concrete walls just as effectively as he'd bound her to wooden bedposts.

You will learn to crave this.

Another echo of his voice in her head, and she covered her ears like she could block it out. Twisting in the sheets, she buried her face in the pillow, still waiting for him to return.

This was just a new game for him.

Taking her down from the ropes? Feeding her warm soup and cold juice? Bringing her to this room and telling her to sleep? It wasn't real. She had never apologized for ripping all of the terrifying *things* from the walls in this room, for tearing his poster to pieces with the aid of some of those things. Had never expressed regret for pulling apart his cabinet of tools and dildos and gags and cuffs.

And that meant this room could *not* be a reward.

It was just a different vista for her torture.

He had cleaned up the room. Put everything back in its place. Replaced the poster with a pristine one. Erased the violence of the morning like it had never existed. She had wanted to destroy it all, but even the broken drawers were somehow back in the cabinet. It was a false sheen of perfection, just like his suits. And just like him...

underneath the pretty veneer it was all rotting. Corrupted. Evil.

This is not a reward, she reminded herself. Said it again, and again, and again in her mind so that the softness of the mattress wouldn't lull her into comfort.

Not like the reminder was necessary, Beth was terrified to sleep. Terrified she might wake up to a new horror, a fresh creation from his devious mind as he tried his best to make her obedient. To make her a *thing*.

Turning over again, she focused on the pale light spilling from the open bathroom door. He had turned off all of the lights when he had left her on the bed, pulling the sheets over her as if he were tucking her in, but as soon as the door had closed, she had walked to it. Tested the handle and found it locked. *Always locked.* So, she had turned on the bathroom light, angled the door so she could see, and crawled back under the sheets.

The glinting glass from the cameras caught the light, but they had faded into the background of her mind. If she thought too much about them, she would worry again about how comfortable she had grown in her nakedness — so she didn't.

She refused to think about them and the faceless monsters behind them.

Refused to look at the spotless room, at the pristine linens that were free of the reddish stains she'd left on them. Instead, she focused on her wrists. The bruises, the dark spots where she had rubbed the skin raw against rope and leather, the places where she had bled in pinprick dots. Her ankles matched. Her knees and shins were mottled with bruises. Those were things he couldn't erase. Couldn't clean up.

How much can you take before you snap?

His voice again. A question he had asked her the day before, just before he'd spread the bar between her legs a little wider, forcing her pussy against the thin beam of wood she straddled. Pelvic bone crushing sensitive flesh as her body weight rested on it, arms bound behind her back, toes aching as she tried to lift herself the tiniest amount. It had hurt, and then hurt worse. There always seemed to be *worse.*

Pain. Always more pain.

The torment on the wood had been in this room, as had so many other terrible things. Soft bed or not, he planned to give her more of the same. Every single day.

She had no idea how much time had passed since he had taken her. How many days. No clocks, no windows, no daylight, no night. Just the lights, on or off. Just the erratic meals, or hollow hunger. Just time spent alone, or time with him.

How much can you take before you snap?

How much can you take?

How much?

She didn't know. The questions spiraled inside her, edged like sharp knives, piercing her with tiny nicks. Death by a thousand cuts. She didn't know how much more of this she could take, how many more hours, days... but she wasn't broken yet. Wouldn't stop fighting until she couldn't anymore.

To stop fighting, to give in, *that* would be the worst thing of all — and she wouldn't do it.

––––––

The bed shifted, her arm tugged out from under the pillow, and Beth groaned as she fought to stay asleep. In sleep there had been an endless peace, like sinking to the bottom of a warm, dark pool. Serene and quiet. But she felt strong fingers press her wrist against something, and then the crackling rip of Velcro tore her eyes open.

A dark shape above her, backlit by the light from the bathroom, but when he lifted his head... he looked wrong. Shoulders too broad, hair too short.

"You're awake. Good."

No. His voice was wrong too. Panic flared to life inside her, finding new fuel as he pressed a knee to the bed to lean forward and wrap a black strip around her thigh. "Stop," she half-demanded, half-begged the stranger above her.

Because that's what he was, a stranger. A new threat.

She tried to raise her hands but found that one was tethered to the thigh closest to him by a matching black strip. Her confusion allowed him to stretch the Velcro and attach it to her thigh. "NO!" she shouted, desperate, sitting up to rip at the slick fabric around her other wrist, but he pulled her hand away, grip too strong to fight.

Had he sold her already? Was this it?

"Please, don't..." she begged as he forced her arm to her thigh, joining it to the wide strap by the attached cuff, leaving her defenseless. No matter how she twisted her hands, she couldn't break free, couldn't bend her fingers enough to get a grip on the Velcro to pull it open.

The man walked away from her, towards the door, and for a moment she thought he might leave — but then the lights came on. Vicious, too bright. She flinched away from them, dropped back on the bed, clenching her eyes tight.

"Beth." It was the surprising use of her name that made her look at him again. Stunned by the sound of it, because there had been so many degrading names spoken by the other one in the days he'd had her, but never her name. Only once, that first night, in this bed.

"Please…" She didn't even know why she whispered it, why the word escaped her lips so soft and pathetic. It was ridiculous to think he would help her, he had just tethered her wrists to her thighs, but she still looked up at him with foolish hope.

"Do you know who I am?" he asked. Attractive like the other one, but more warm. More human. There was a subtle smile on his lips, a curve to his mouth that rang true as his eyes roamed over her skin.

She shook her head slowly, hoping to delay whatever was coming next.

"Interesting." He pulled off his jacket and tossed it onto the chair in the corner. Then his shirt followed, and she held her breath. Carved abs, a sculpted chest, broad shoulders and strong arms. The flicker of attraction to his body was short-lived, because he stepped forward to brush his fingers over the strap holding her right wrist down. "You haven't submitted."

Her body jolted, fire filling her mind with purpose. "I won't."

A chuckle rumbled up from his chest. "You will."

"*No*," she hissed.

"Are you sure?" he asked as he slid his hand under her head, threading his fingers through her hair until he slowly formed a fist. Sparks of pain lit up across her scalp as he used his grip to pull her into a sitting position.

She felt like a doll. Poseable and vacant, arms trapped at her sides. But she had already made up her mind — one monster or another — she wasn't giving in. "I'm sure," she answered, prepared for pain, but his fist in her hair only leaned her forward a little further... and then he climbed onto the bed behind her.

His knees rose up on either side as he settled against the headboard, and then he pulled her back against his firm chest. Hot skin on skin. It was the first time she'd felt it here. The other one always kept his clothes on, only unzipping his pants when he wanted to use her, but this one had his bare chest to her back, and... it was strangely *comforting*.

Which was wrong.

Nothing about this was okay.

"Don't hurt me," she mumbled. Almost a question, almost a plea.

"Don't *make* me hurt you, Beth. You have so many decisions to make, so many options..." His strong hands brushed up her arms, squeezing occasionally as if he were casually massaging her.

"About what?" she whispered, shuddering as his hands slid to the front of her shoulders, pressing her back to his front.

The man's lips were against her ear when he answered, the barest hint of scruff on his cheek scratching her skin. "About what happens to you next."

Fear trickled down her spine, ice-cold despite his body heat — and he was so *warm*. Even his voice was filled with heat, hunger as his hands slid lower, tracing the outsides of her breasts before moving to her arms to follow them down. Then, he started the path over.

Squeezing, brushing, tickling when his touch grew too light.

Finally, she swallowed and made herself speak. "What happens next?"

"Up to you."

"I want to leave."

He laughed quietly, his chest shaking behind her, the low sound of his voice against her neck. "*That* is not one of the options."

Jerking at the sleek, soft cuffs attached to her thighs, she spat, "Then what are my fucking options?"

His fingers tightened painfully on one nipple, twisting hard as the shocking pain of it made her back arch against him, useless cries escaping between clenched teeth. When he finally let go, she was panting, fists clenched tight — and then he pressed a kiss to her neck. Brushing her hair out of the way, he did it again, and again. Licking, teasing nips of his teeth along the side of her throat as his thumb rubbed soothing circles over her tortured bud. "Don't make me hurt you. Be respectful and I can make it so much easier."

Beth was stiff, tense, trapped against his body, and her muscles locked even further when he wound an arm under hers and slipped his hand between her thighs. "Don't…" she pleaded, but quickly bit her lip, hoping to avoid more pain.

"Tell me the truth…" His fingers delved lower, parting her lips to seek out her clit, teasing with delicate touches. "Has he ever made you come?"

"*No.*" Shaking her head, she leaned away when he started to trail kisses from her shoulder up her throat again. It was too intimate, too gentle, too much like an actual lover.

Well, except for the cuffs, and the poster of rules hanging directly across from them like a fucking taunt from the other one.

Tell me the rules.

His voice was back in her head, but this one had his fingers moving with sinister precision over the bundle of nerves between her legs. Rubbing in small circles. Her hips twitched and she flinched, forcing her eyes shut like she could block out the sensations as easily as she could the sight of the damn poster.

It was impossible.

Impossible that *anything* could feel good in this nightmare, and impossible to ignore the wetness he gathered with one sinful sweep of his middle finger over her entrance.

Tracing her damnation back up to her clit, he used her own wetness to ease his movements. As he settled into an easy pattern, two fingers moving incessantly, he spoke softly. "I said you have options, Beth, would you like to know what they are?"

Something brittle inside her was spider-webbing with cracks. Each flicker of sensation from his touch was confirmation that she wasn't damaged beyond repair, that she could still feel — and yet it was somehow worse than anything the other one had done. "I don't care," she answered, clenching her jaw and breathing deep to push back the low thrum.

"I think you do." The pressure of his fingers increased, tempo building with it, and she pressed back into his chest on instinct trying to escape. It was his quiet laugh that froze her once more. "This feels nice, doesn't it? Don't you want me to keep going?"

He kissed her neck again and she jerked away, but he grabbed her hair in his free hand and wrenched her head to the other side.

"Beth, you're not behaving." It was a warning, coupled with the sharper nip of his teeth against her bared shoulder, but she wasn't going to submit just because he had heat pooling between her thighs and tremors of pleasure battling it out with the fear already buzzing in her veins.

"I'm not obedient, or didn't your buddy mention that?"

"He is not my friend." His fist tightened in her hair, sparks of pain radiating across her scalp as he increased the fervor of his fingers on her clit.

Fuck, why does it feel good? It shouldn't feel good.

"He is my partner in this enterprise, but it doesn't matter.

I can make you be obedient. I can *make* you do so many things… wouldn't it be easier if you just gave in?" Nibbling on her neck, he focused on her clit with confident swirls of his fingers, her wetness growing, inner walls clenching around nothing. "You can choose to obey me, and I will make you feel good. Choose to submit, to be a good girl. Everything will be easier for you… I promise."

"I don't want to," she whispered, voice breaking. Straining against the urge to slip into what he offered, to submerge herself in the waves of pleasure between her thighs, the devious touch that had her hips subtly rocking.

"You know what disobedience brings you, Beth." Lips to her ear, his other arm wrapped around her waist to pull her tighter against him, erection pressed into her spine. "Don't make me hurt you," he whispered quietly, just for her.

So much emotion in his voice, in *him*.

The other one was solid ice, animated stone, an empty shell.

This one was full color. There was hunger in him, warmth in his body and his touch. He was good at this, her body relaxing despite her best efforts to stay apart. To stay strong. To ignore the potential for delirium that he teased from her.

"Ask for permission before you come, Beth." Those words jarred her, made her whimper, struggle, but he held her tight to his body.

"I won't come." *I can't. I can't. I can't.*

What would it mean to orgasm here? In this place? Would

it feel like an orgasm anywhere else? Would it be a momentary gasp of freedom?

Or would it drive her further into this hell… leave her emptier than when he'd begun, than when the other one had raped her the first night.

"I don't want this," she said softly, but his laughter came again, shaking against her back as he slid one finger inside. The invasion made tears prick her eyes, wrists pulling uselessly at the cuffs that didn't hurt but were no less effective.

"Are you sore?" he asked, sliding a second finger inside to stretch her, waking up the ache his partner had left behind in the early hours of the morning. "I know he likes to fuck you hard, that's the only way he knows… but I can make you like it, enjoy it."

"Please don't—"

"Open your legs. Now." The anger in his voice made her open her eyes, only to see his wrist trapped between her thighs. When she hesitated, he reached forward and pulled one knee to the side while he used his feet to pull hers wide. "Every time you try to close your legs that's another belt stroke. Understand?"

"No!"

His grip tightened on the skin above her knee, two fingers thrusting hard. "I will take my belt to your ass, your thighs, so that you remember that closing your legs to me, or my partner, is unacceptable. Does *that* make things clear?"

"Please… just stop…" she begged, legs shaking as he slid her wetness back to her clit and focused on it for an excruciatingly long minute of forced pleasure. Warmth and lust moving through her body like a heady buzz. Muting the fear in her nerves, quelling the panic in her veins, until all that existed was the steady thrum of his touch. Each swirl over her clit another confusing crack in the brittle barrier she'd formed against reality.

"Am I clear?" he asked again, slipping his fingers inside her, curving his fingers to stroke her g-spot and make her body jolt forward, legs jerking inward. "That counts."

"Please don't make me—" She couldn't say it aloud. *Don't make me do this. Don't make me come. Don't make me enjoy this for even a moment. Stop, stop, stop…*

Laughter. Real, low, male laughter behind her that made the tears roll down her cheeks as his arm tightened across her ribs, holding her against his chest even as she struggled to writhe. Hips wanton and desperate to meet the next sinful sweep of his fingers. To feel something nice, something good, no matter the price.

She opened her eyes to see his hand moving, digits buried inside her. Unwelcome, yet bringing her the only comfort she'd received here.

Threats and pleasure.

"Do you want me to *make* you like it? Is that what you need, Beth?" His voice was a purr, directly against her ear, and it fed down her spine like a rumble. Vibrating the space between her thighs as he stroked expertly, teasing her to the edge as she struggled to keep her legs apart. To fight back the orgasm.

I can't do this. I won't do this. I won't enjoy this.

"No."

"You're so wet. Has he ever made you wet like this?" The sound of him thrusting his fingers in and out of her made her flinch. Soaked, *squelching* sounds that made her shudder in shame and embarrassing pleasure.

Beth drew her lip between her teeth and bit down hard, feeling the burning ache spread across her jaw as she fought it. Fought against her own body as it betrayed her, spilling liquid heat down to the bedding beneath her, cloaking his fingers in her dripping duplicity. There was a new tension tightening like a knot at the bottom of her spine, wrapping taut, coiling with each new slip of his touch inside her. Cracking the brittle barrier further every time he slid free to torment her clit with a new wave of pleasure. Forcing her body to respond, react.

"Just call me *Master* and you can come, Beth." His voice against her ear was harried. He was breathing harder, aroused, tainted with lust and need — things his rigid partner was not capable of — but humanity didn't make him good. It just made his requests all the more monstrous.

He knew exactly what he was devouring.

"No," she refused again. Holding onto the only power they'd left her. They could take what they wanted, they had made that painfully clear, but this? Her permission? Her submission? Her agreement?

That she would never give.

"You better ask permission then, or I'm *really* going to hurt you." His fingers started to move in earnest, aggressive thrusts, strong strokes inside that pressed her g-spot and made her body buckle no matter how much she fought.

"I won't come," she swore.

"Yes, you will." And then he did his best to bend her to his will, to break her, playing her body with an expertise that had her whining, whimpering — and, *fuck*, she was even moaning softly — as her foolish body collapsed under the onslaught of pleasure. The teasing of nerves. Delirious lightning crackled over her skin, plaguing her veins with an urge to dive into oblivion… escape.

Why did it have to feel this good? This tempting?

She wanted to believe this tingling ferocity was the same as the electric shocks in the cement room where his partner had chained her down. Wanted to equate the two in her mind so she could push the ecstasy away, remove herself from it, destroy it.

But it wasn't the same.

It was a new torture, and as much as she wanted to pretend it wasn't affecting her, she could feel the sweat on her skin, the delirious buzz that had her breaths shortening — and his lips on her throat were not helping.

Too personal. Too real.

Too *not* like the man he called his partner.

Creeping like implacable vines over all of her barriers, tearing them to pieces, holding the shreds of her sanity so she wouldn't feel them hit the earth, so she couldn't scream at the void of what used to be her pride.

Beth was shaking, shivering, so close to an orgasm that her muscles were nothing more than tremors and heat. *Warmth.* For once, she was sweating, not shivering, and there was no pain. Only pleasure, corrupting satisfaction that beckoned her to the edge of darkness like a van with candy that promised a permanent escape from everything — but it was all poisoned. Every blissful inch of his fingers sliding inside her traitorous wetness was tainted. By this room, by him, by his actions, his partner's.

Nothing was real.

And, yet, it didn't matter, because the physical response was unavoidable.

"Say it. Call me Master." A sinful growl against her ear, delectable. So easy to lean against his hard, muscular chest and give in. So tempting.

So close.

"NO!" she screamed. Beth pulled desperately against the soft cuffs that tethered her arms to her thighs, focusing on the hot tears rolling down her cheeks instead of the heat pulsing between her thighs.

Ignore the pleasure. Ignore it. Fight it. *Please.*

The man slid his fingers deep, curving, tapping at the crucial spot at her core that had her body bowing forward, unable to argue biology — and then she came all over his hand. Light exploded at the ends of her nerve endings, mind blissfully empty for a moment, so drowned in biochemical pleasure that she forgot everything. The room, the man, the poster of rules, and the wall of twisted torture devices. It was a mental escape, a trapdoor out of hell, but as it faded she tumbled into something so much worse.

Slick and wet as the tears on her cheeks, but equally as pointless.

Gently, he pulled his fingers from her and forced them into her gasping mouth, pushing in as he caught her jaw in the other hand. Smarter than his partner, unable to bite down as he held her still and slid the damning taste of her arousal over her tongue. Then he pushed too far, gagging her, and she choked around the flavor of her shame. "Say it," he demanded again from behind her, skull trapped against his collarbone with his fingers buried deep.

"Nyyoo—" Beth tried her best to refuse past his hand, accepting the pain that was to come. Welcoming it on the discordant edge of her forced orgasm, and his growl accompanied by his next words only confirmed it.

"Oh, I'm going to hurt you, whore." Tearing his fingers from her mouth, he shoved her forward on the bed. Weakly landing on her side as he moved away, left the bed, but she had no misconception that he was done with her. This pleasurable, horrible interlude was only the beginning.

With a jerk, he flipped her to her stomach, unstrapping her wrists from her thighs. She heard the crackling as he pressed them together behind her back. Again, they were wrapped tight, but just as she tried to worm her fingers under the velcro he wound a strip all the way around.

No chance.

Hands under her thighs, he yanked her to the edge of the bed, hips bent, and then she heard the rattling fastenings of his belt. The whisper of leather leaving the dark pants he wore terrified her, and then — *CRACK!*

White hot pain in a vicious stripe across her ass, too shocked to scream with the first one, but the next loud snap of leather landed on her thighs and she managed it. Voice breaking as she screamed, begged into the sheet that smelled of her arousal as lines of fire blistered her ass and thighs.

Over and over and over.

Agony crashed in on the heels of too much pleasure, suffocated the memory of her orgasm, drowning it along with her hopes of ever getting out.

"SAY IT! CALL ME MASTER!" he roared behind her, but her ears were buzzing from the pain, body shaking as she tried to process the feel of her heartbeat in the flesh he'd brutalized. Tears and drool soaked the sheet beneath her cheek, but she stayed silent.

Giving in won't make this stop. It won't.

It's a lie, a fucking lie, it's always a lie.

"Bitch." The vulgar growl, and the tinkling sound of metal fixtures, overwhelmed her ragged breaths for the brief moment before he struck again. Excruciating, so much worse than the electricity. It didn't end, didn't stop, and left more than sore muscles behind.

He was hitting her harder now, the pain rising to some place inside where it could go no further, blurring into white noise in her head that silenced her screams, her cries, her incoherent pleading. Everything vibrated with the same tone, the same peak of suffering that he was now drawing out into a plateau meant for her destruction.

Thoughts were born and died before she could process them, catching only bits and pieces. Hints of her dissolving hope, her boiling hatred for them both, her psychotic temptation to give in and be whatever doll they wanted if only it would make him drop the fucking belt.

It was for the best that she couldn't think straight. Couldn't make her voice form more than low grunts on the heels of each new lash over already destroyed flesh.

When he stopped again, her head swam. Barely reacting as he wound his fist in her hair and bowed her backwards, a gurgle of strain slipping from her as his knees created a place between hers. "Last chance for mercy, slut."

Mercy?

Her brain was useless, but that one word was written in blood on the inside of it.

There would be no mercy here.

I am not merciful.

The other one's voice made it through the fog in her head even though he wasn't in this room. Both of them torturing her simultaneously, but there was only one with his hands on her at the moment.

When he laughed, her body twitched, an autonomic surge of useless fight or flight… and then he was inside her. Still miserably wet, the stroke stretched her open until he bottomed out, hips slamming hard against her bruised and welted ass. Pinprick spikes of pain inside the white noise, another inelegant grunt from her throat as he wrapped his hands around her hips and slid almost completely out, only to force himself deep again.

It was pure aggression. Animalistic as he thrust over and over, making her ache inside as well as out, pressing finger-shaped bruises into her hips. She tried not to react to the pounding of his cock, the way his hard flesh pushed against her inner walls, but he was at the perfect angle to punish her g-spot with pleasure — and there was no doubt that this *was* punishment. The slow burn of arousal was breaking through the white noise, bringing her back to her body, connecting her to the aches and sinful tremors in equal measure.

Beth whimpered, digging her nails into her palms, biting the inside of her cheek, *anything* to stop this from happening again. She hated herself for squeezing him inside her, for groaning into the bedding, trapped on some kind of terrible autopilot that clung to the rising tide of lust in her veins.

"See?" he gloated, jerking her backwards onto his cock. "I can hurt you, or I can make you like it, slave."

Clenching her eyes tight, she prayed for the detachment to return, for the white noise to fill her once more, but it was his fingers that came back. Pressed against her clit as he leaned over her, the heat of his breath on her back, and then there was only pleasure. It stormed down the aches and pains in her muscles and skin, making her hips buck as he made each stroke count. Hard, powerful, forcing her to accept him and every tremor that threatened an orgasm.

Jagged cuts of lightning through her mind, pure bliss and ecstasy.

This was so much better. So much better than the pain, than the cold, than the other one's icy emptiness.

"Just call me Master and I can make you feel like this every day." Heavy, panted words, and as he focused his touch on her clit again she felt her resolve crumbling. That pathetic barrier she had constructed ground to dust, blown away by the next tempting drive of his cock.

Master.

Such a simple word, a simple thing. She didn't even have to

mean it. She *never* had to mean it. Never had to pretend this was who she really was.

He pushed inside her and held deep, still teasingly rubbing her clit, holding her on the edge, but it was when his other hand slipped through the collar at the back of her neck that everything shuddered.

It was a wake-up call. She wore a collar.

This would *never* be okay. She would *never* submit. She would *never* call either of these bastards Master. No matter how good they made her feel. No matter how much they made her hurt.

I'm a person. I'm still me. Fuck. *I'm going to come.*

The orgasm had crept past the ruins of her self-control as she'd focused on the collar, on reminding herself of her promises, but now it was threatening in blinding colors. Thighs trembling, body tense, she tried to stop it, but he swiveled his hips and thrust hard just as he pinched her clit — and she was gone.

Moaning into the bed as molten light careened through her nervous system and washed away reality once more. It felt good, too incredible after he'd hurt her so much. Her body was desperate for the pleasure, devouring it like it was starving and he was still thrusting as her pussy clenched and squeezed in waves, dragging out the orgasm until she was limp and sweating. Gasping, mewling, heart hammering a staccato on the inside of her ribs.

He slid from the soaking mess between her thighs — all her, because she had never felt him come. A hard slap on her ass woke up the welts, pain making the orgasm stutter. "What did I say about asking permission?"

I'm sorry.

That was what the other one would want to hear, even if she didn't mean it. This one? He only wanted one word from her.

"Greedy little whore." His large palms squeezed her backside, making her whimper as the welts protested and he pulled her cheeks apart. "You like it, don't you... you wanna take it? You wanna take my cock some more?"

Beth arched as he pressed against her ass, shaking her head, but his hands found her hips again and he ripped her open in one vicious stroke. She screamed against the bed, pleading for him to stop, but he pulled back and it felt like a hot knife being drawn out, and then re-sheathed as he thrust forward. An impossible pain.

"Oh, *fuck*, yes." He groaned as he tore her apart, hips pistoning with unrelenting strokes. "Take it, slut. This is all you're meant for, all you're good for. Just a set of fucking holes."

Sobbing, back muscles spasming, Beth tried to stop herself from screaming again, but it was useless. She screamed for him, again and again.

Pain, panic, all pleasure gone like smoke.

Nothing but agony.

And then he forced himself deep, teeth clamping down on her flesh as he came. Squirming, she tried not to tighten down because it only hurt worse, sobbing as the torment of his bite refused to let her dissolve, pass out, escape.

He pulled out, ripping her head up by her hair, and she saw the rage still simmering in his eyes, even with the manic smile on his lips. "Was it good for you?" he asked, and then he spat into her face.

She felt something crumple inside just before he dropped her back to the bed. The dull sounds of him gathering his clothes faded into the background noise of her pain, and when the door finally shut Beth let the tremors in her body takeover.

It took a few tries, a few weak screams into the sheet, but she finally lifted one knee onto the bed and managed to shift her body completely onto it. Arms still behind her back, she ignored the meager throb of her shoulder as she curled into a ball on her side. This was definitely hell, and there were two devils, not one.

And each day she was discovering a new level of suffering. A new low.

Accepting a new thought as an absolute truth…

I'm going to die here.

TEN

Marcus

"Well, that went well." Anthony spoke from the door, his eyes glued to the phone in his hands.

"Fuck you," Marcus growled, pouring another inch of scotch before he downed it on a hiss.

A low sound came from his brother, almost a laugh, and his fingers tightened threateningly around the brittle glass. When Anthony walked forward, taking slow measured steps, Marcus forced himself to set the empty drink down before he shattered it, or threw it at the asshole. He stopped about ten feet to his left, as if he could sense the threat, floating at the edge of his peripheral vision. "I'm sure you noticed, but she did *not* call you Master."

"I noticed."

"You know what that means then?" The cold calm of the question only fueled Marcus' rage, hand shaking with it as he grabbed the bottle of scotch and poured again.

Watching the amber liquid splash, he kept his eyes there,

not daring to look at Anthony until he had his temper in check. "Yeah, I do."

A burning swallow, and then another, but it was Anthony's huff of breath that made his muscles twitch.

Raising his eyes, he pointed at him with the hand holding the glass. "You did something to her. I know you did."

"Review the recordings if you think so, but I did exactly as we agreed. I took her down from the suspension, I fed her, and I put her in bed. *For you.*" The casual lift of his shoulder was the only reaction his brother gave. "It's not my fault you failed."

Failed.

The word felt like a punch to the stomach, and he hated him even more. This sonuvabitch was ruining everything, probably *already* ruined everything with his fucked-up techniques. Rage simmered in his blood, still burning through his veins after the defiance the cunt had displayed, and it was all because of Anthony. All of it.

"No one is going to fucking buy her like this!" Marcus shouted, gesturing in the direction of the room where he'd left the bitch bound and crying. "You think anyone wants a slave that won't even call them Master?"

"It has only been a week, we"—he paused, giving his creepy fucking smile as he tilted his head, dead eyes lifting until they were looking at each other—"or rather, *I* still have plenty of time to break her."

"Fuck off."

"That is precisely what I was going to recommend *you* do, Marcus. As I tried to tell you on the phone this evening, your presence tonight was not necessary." Anthony walked over to lean against a leather chair, and when he looked at him again he could sense the satisfaction he took in the next words. "And now your presence is simply not acceptable. We had an agreement after all."

"You're such an asshole. Can I at least sleep here, or do you want me to drive North right fucking now?" Growling, he turned away from the bastard and poured more scotch, swallowing before it even had a chance to breathe.

"That would be irresponsible. You're already drowning your sorrows in liquor, and I'd much prefer you out of a hospital since you've invested so much setting up the alternate location for our customers." He paused, another huff of sound leaving him. "Then you can focus your misguided efforts on your own slave."

"I could have made her say it!" Marcus roared, slamming the empty glass down on the bar cabinet.

"But, you did not."

"She would have said it if you had let me handle her from the beginning!" Running his hand over the short crop of his hair, he cursed and paced across the room, avoiding the alcohol because he knew his brother saw it as weakness. "You've fucking ruined her. YOU have, Anthony. That's the only reason she refused!"

Another barely perceptible shrug was the only reaction he got. No flare of irritation, no flicker of emotion in that stone-cold face. His brother had his phone in his hand, tapping at it with one hand, barely paying attention to him. "She will break. They all do."

"When?" he shouted, feeling his teeth grind when he snapped them back together.

"Eventually."

"Fuck you, Anthony." Fury pounded through his veins, making his blood pulse behind his eyes, heart beating too fast. The orgasm hadn't taken the edge off, it had only fueled it. Even screaming and crying she'd refused to call him Master — what would Anthony do now?

He found himself back at the bar cabinet, one hand on the bottle of scotch, tongue tracing his lower lip as he imagined the smoky taste of his brother's Glenlivet.

"Will another drink really help you?" Anthony asked, and Marcus wrapped his other hand around the glass, fighting the instinct to pour, and drink, and pour again until he could block out his brother's fucking voice. "You're being childish, Marcus."

His grip tightened, the glass shattering under his fist and he ripped his hand back as blood pooled from his thumb. Hissing through his teeth, he ignored the pain and turned to stare at the asshole who supposedly shared DNA with him.

"I'm being *childish*?" Letting his blood swell in his fist, the warm liquid seeping between his fingers to drip to the carpet, Marcus fought the urge to shout again and forced out a laugh.

It was at least entertaining to be ruining what was likely an expensive rug.

Reaching back, he grabbed the open bottle and tilted it up, swallowing a mouthful that burned but left the delicious smoke behind as he breathed out and smiled. "Nothing I did this evening was childish, Anthony, and if she didn't submit to *that*, she's not going to submit after another week, or another month of your torture shit."

"Right… I'm glad you brought up your behavior this evening." Lifting the phone at his side, he angled the screen towards him and it lit up. "Do you remember what you told me on our call?"

"Yeah, I agreed to your fucking bet. You get to finish training this one solo, I stay out of it, and you get *all* the profits. Trust me, I didn't forget."

"Oh, all of that is true. I'm referring to something *else* you said on our call."

"What?" Taking another drink, he leaned back against the bar, listening to the bottles rattle, the shards of glass tinkling on the metal tray as the buzz of alcohol finally started to spread. "You already screwed me over on this. What else is there? Just fucking spit it out, Anthony."

"You claimed you could break her *without* fucking her ass… and then what did you do?"

He laughed. He couldn't help it. He'd actually managed to take something from his brother, and it felt *good*. "Is that what this is about? The fact that I fucked her in the ass?" Grinning, he thought back to the smooth curve of her back, the swell of her hips under his hands, the sight of her wrists bound in dark cuffs. "Did you watch, Anthony? She came all over my cock, and then she screamed when I took her ass for the first time. Screamed and begged me."

Anthony's mouth twitched, eyes dropping to the phone for a second, and Marcus felt victory for one fleeting moment — and then his asshole of a brother smiled.

"Yes, I saw, and I just received the confirmation that fifty-thousand dollars was just transferred from your account to mine. A penalty, for breaking the parameters of our wager."

"WHAT?" Marcus took a few steps towards him, palm wet with blood, and he wanted to make him bleed, to rip him apart, but Anthony raised the phone up again.

"Actions have consequences, Marcus. This will be a good lesson for you to learn, especially if we plan to operate separate, but connected, businesses." Tilting the phone to and fro, he continued, "And I can always transfer more if you feel the need to act out."

Fuck.

He wanted to hit him. Hard. Wanted to punch him in his fucking face until they looked nothing alike. This didn't have a thing to do with the girl, this was just Anthony reminding him who the fuck was in charge.

Another fucking power play, and he'd walked right into it.

When would he learn not to bet against his brother? The man only made bets he knew he would win, which meant he *had* to have done something to the girl. Drugged her, hurt her, threatened her. He'd go over the recordings piece by piece and find it.

Forcing another swallow of the expensive liquor, he tried to calm down, to focus. "Fifty-thousand for her ass, Anthony? That seems like a bit much."

"It's also for the bruises from your little temper tantrum with the belt. Our customers tend to prefer blank slates for their own marks."

Marcus snorted. "She'll heal from those long before *you* get her to call you Master."

"Well, *when* I get her to call me Master, we will see. But you will not be here for it." Tucking his phone in his pocket, Anthony moved towards the door. "I expect you out in the morning."

"No reason for me to stay, is there?"

"No." He didn't even turn around when he answered, just opened the door and walked out into the hall, letting it fall shut behind him with a clap. The automatic lock clicking into place let him relax, and he opened his sticky fist to look at the cut on his thumb.

Not deep, but it hadn't stopped bleeding.

He could fix this. He would fix all of it.

Taking the bottle with him, he walked to the door and opened it with his bloody hand, leaving dark, smudged fingerprints on the keypad and handle. Ruining the pristine sheen his brother kept over everything.

In his room he had a first-aid kit, and his old computer setup. He could bandage his thumb and spend the rest of the night getting drunk and pouring over the recordings until he found the exact moment when Anthony had fucked him over.

Then he could take Beth for himself and show them all who was better at breaking slaves.

ELEVEN

Anthony

Anthony watched as she pressed herself forward against the cool, concrete wall. Wrists in dark cuffs, arms spread wide, linked to the hard points high above her head. He had always enjoyed this design. The chains allowed him to adjust based on their height so he could make them stretch. Even now, she was up on her toes, calves shaking from the strain, round ass catching the harsh overhead lights.

It had been two weeks of things like this. Creative punishments, mind games, but the girl seemed more defiant than ever.

She'd even told him to kill her.

So ridiculous.

First, slaves were not allowed to make demands.

Second, he didn't believe for an instant the girl truly wanted to die. No living thing did. It was hard-wired into their biology to survive — and no matter what he did to her, she would always crave another breath.

Most importantly, this was a business, and good businessmen never invested time and money in something only to abandon it at the first hint of hardship.

He just needed to be rougher with her. Make her suffer more.

Running the leather of the whip over his palm he focused on the handful of bright red lines across her upper back and shoulders. "What are you, girl?"

Her body jerked, twisted a little as she shifted her weight between her feet, but she didn't answer. Fingers wrapped tight around the chains, she was either extraordinarily strong, or impressively stupid.

"Silence is defiance. Do you need another reminder?" Uncoiling the whip, he let it hang to the floor once more. Waiting, watching as he adjusted his grip and moved to the side again, letting her hear his footsteps — but she still didn't speak.

Lifting his arm, he swung forward, hearing the whip snap against her flesh a second before a guttural cry left her lips, soft whimpers following. Another bright red line formed, and he wondered if she knew he could strike so much harder. Could make those lines purple, could make her bleed.

"What are you, girl?" he repeated, and it irked him. He'd asked the same question so many times and he despised repeating himself. A waste of time and energy. "Answer me."

"*No,*" she whispered between harsh breaths, her jaw muscles twitching as she pressed her teeth together again.

Another crack of the whip, harder, and she gasped before she screamed. This line was going to be darker, a lovely reddish-purple. It probably hurt, a lot, but he had never been whipped so he didn't know exactly what it felt like.

"FUCK YOU!" the girl screamed, voice breaking at the end of the expletive as she dissolved into whines, rattling the chains with her twists and tugs. It was a pretty sight from the side. Round breasts brushing the concrete, flat stomach twisting above wiggling hips.

The customers are absolutely enjoying this.

Walking over to the table he set the whip down and picked up the bar gag. She was still breathing harshly when he approached, refusing to look at him as she leaned her forehead against the wall. There was no doubt in his mind that it was her exhaustion, and not some last-minute attempt at obedience that kept her eyes averted.

She was disobedient to the core, but he had something else after the whipping to break her a little further.

"Open your mouth." *That* drew her attention, head twisting to look over her shoulder at him, and he lifted the gag so she could see it. Brown eyes went wide, and her jaw tightened.

Anthony was somewhat fascinated by her. Normally, there was so much pleading and begging, especially when he used the whip — a boorish, yet painful implement if there ever was one — but she was still cursing. Still brazenly refusing to submit, and nowhere near breaking.

Weaving his fingers into her hair he ripped her head back,

the natural gasp of breath into her lungs opening her jaw, and he shoved the leather bit between her teeth before she could correct it. It only took a moment to wind the leather behind her head, under the ponytail he had roughly pulled together to keep it off her back.

She sputtered curses around it, still loud, but less intelligible.

Much better.

"I did tell you what would happen if you cursed at me again, remember, slut?" He stroked her hair, smiling when she pulled away from him. "Ready for the rest of your whipping?"

A garbled stream came from her, and he could almost pick out the obscenities as he returned to the whip. The leather was still warm from his hand, a comfortable hold.

"If you would like to answer my questions from this morning, or address me properly, simply snap your fingers. Otherwise, we will finish this part of your punishment." Anthony watched as the muscles in her back twitched, her legs bending and straightening. Preparing for the pain.

It wouldn't help her, of course, but he allowed her the moment anyway.

Sometimes, he was too generous.

Rearing his arm back, he snapped the whip across her shoulders, reveling in the scream as his cock twitched. Still sated from before he'd chained her up, but he enjoyed it anyway. Another lash, harder, and her back bowed before she pressed her body into the concrete.

Darker.

That line was already a deep purple, and he listened to her sob, the slurping sounds around the gag as she tried to avoid drooling.

In a moment none of that would matter to her.

The whip arced through the air so fast his eyes couldn't track it, trusting his skill to land it where he wanted, and over and over it did. Practice makes perfect, or so they say, and though he'd prefer the marks to be more evenly spaced, they were still grouped carefully across the top of her back.

Eyes roving to her ass and thighs he admired the clean expanse of flesh, the belt marks having faded from his brother's interlude with her, and he smiled. Shifting his feet, he angled lower and the whip cracked at a diagonal across her ass.

A new scream, guttural sobbing. She hadn't expected him to strike somewhere new.

Anthony paused a moment to enjoy her despair, the hiss of her breaths around the gag, the whimpers, the occasional sucking in as she fought to swallow the saliva he knew was pooling in her mouth. He *could* have put her in a ball gag, but that was for shorter durations than he planned to have her in this one.

Tonight, he would torture her in new ways.

But first, the whipping. Two more lashes across her ass, dark ones that drew out the most desperate screams of pain, and then he added another across her shoulders. The girl bucked, crying, and he saw the first string of drool spill from her lips. It glinted in the light as it spilled onto her breasts, and she whined, sputtering as she gave in and let more flow.

How many emails had he received requesting a whipping?

Too many to count at the moment, but he looked forward to reviewing the live cam views on this session. It had lasted long enough that some of the customers would have reached out to others they knew, encouraged them to access it.

Which meant she needed to perform.

"Want to snap your fingers, slave?" He taunted, moving forward to run his hand across the welts on her ass, squeezing hard to turn her soft whimpering into another pain-filled scream. Leaning closer he spoke almost directly into her ear, "If you do it, I might even stop. Isn't that what you want?"

She jerked violently against the cuffs, anger suffusing her incoherent shouts, he even thought he heard a garbled *fuck you* in the mess — but she didn't snap her fingers.

It was like she knew what he really wanted in that moment. As perfunctory as it would be for her to break now, to submit, it would be so disappointing. He wanted to hurt her more, wanted her to scream more, wanted to break her down into component parts until he could reassemble her into something marketable.

Which, at this rate, would take so much time.

And he planned to appreciate each and every moment of her destruction.

Moving to the opposite side of her, he rolled the handle of the whip in his fingers, and then gripped it. His muscles twitched in anticipation, cock hardening again as he caught the sheen of his come on her thighs. She was already a slave, already a *thing*, she just hadn't accepted it yet.

The next whip strike across her ass crisscrossed a previous one and she wailed, one foot lifting off the floor like she could block the pain, and then he struck her upper back. She arched, head angled back as she sobbed, and he wondered what she was feeling.

Was there fear in that complex soup of anger and pain? Did she know he could draw blood with the whip? Was she waiting for it?

A visual of crimson streaks rolling down her back filled his mind, and for a moment he even felt tempted. It would just take a little more strength behind the whip to cut flesh like butter. He could tear her to ribbons and listen to her weak screams until she blacked out. Something about the idea was tempting, despite the inherent mess of the blood and the inevitable risk of infection and scarring.

No.

Damaging the merchandise was foolish, and he was never foolish. That was Marcus' territory. Impulsive and imprudent. Eventually she would need to make him money, and while the whip marks were getting darker, they *would* heal without lasting scars.

He had waited too long between strikes with his internal musing. Her breaths were evening out, she wasn't even sobbing anymore despite the occasional sniffle.

If he couldn't make her bleed, he'd just make her suffer.

Lifting his arm, he brought the whip down hard over her

upper back, then her ass. Back, ass, ass, back, again and again, and then, just as she was screaming herself hoarse, he landed the whip high on her thighs. The girl's legs gave out as she sobbed weakly, hanging by her wrists from the cuffs — an added pain of her own making, but he didn't want her breaking something.

Walking forward he wrapped the whip around her throat and used it to pull her back up, aided by his grip around her waist. She choked, coughed, sputtered against the gag as he tightened the whip, and his cock strained at his zipper.

"Do you want to submit yet?" he asked, watching her hands for any hint of an attempted snap.

Nothing.

He hadn't planned to fuck her again, but there was nothing like screaming, or the desperate choking sounds coming out of her now, to make him hard. With her life in his hands, she was as pliable as she needed to be, too weak to stand on her own... but she wasn't even trying to snap her fingers — and he had been so patient. Given her so many chances.

Anthony had refused to fuck her ass so soon after Marcus' hasty actions, wanting to wait until the right moment, and now felt perfect. Dropping the whip, he held on to her with one arm around her waist and unlinked one of the cuffs with the other. Her sudden intake of breath spoke of the hope she felt, the hope that the punishment was over, but he only moved the connector farther down the chain and then locked the cuff in place again.

She sobbed, the jerk of her body against his a clear

indication that this was the right decision. The right moment.

With the second cuff shifted down he was able to pull her away from the wall, to bend her forward, and she braced her palms on it, garbling pleas through the gag. He could hear a broken '*please*', the barely perceptible versions of '*no*' and '*don't*', but her refusals only made him smile because none of them were the answers to his questions.

The girl had not admitted she was a slave, had not called him Master, had not submitted.

"You understand what this means, girl. More punishment." Keeping one arm around her waist, he opened his belt, his pants and zipper, pushing them down as he forced her legs wider. It strained her arms, forced her shoulders to twist, but none of that mattered as he freed his cock and slid inside her hot cunt, still wet with the mix of the two of them. She hadn't come, but he had, and her body's defenses had made her more than wet enough.

Another contribution of his training.

Tightening around him, squeezing, she whimpered as his pants scraped over the whip marks. He moved inside her slowly, letting her believe for a moment that this was all he wanted from her. The girl started to relax, and he knew she was separating from this like she had so many times before.

It would be a short-lived reprieve.

He thrust a few more times, lubricating, before he pulled out and moved his cock to her ass. Body contorting, she whined as she tried to pull away, but his arm around her waist stopped it. She was so weak compared to him, helpless even without the cuffs. He could have done this a hundred times over, could have done it without wetting his cock inside her, but with her gagged and still crying from the pain of the whip? *This* was the moment to take her ass.

"Have you realized yet that there's nothing you can do to stop me?" he asked, watching her ribs expand and contract as she stayed silent. Defiant.

She was practically begging to be punished.

Unlike his brother, he slowly pressed against her tight ring of muscles. Waited for her keening whine to rise, for her body to shudder, her panic to peak before he twitched his hips and forced the head of his cock inside her. *So tight.*

"I can do anything I want with you, because I am your Master whether you say the word or not. And when I sell you, it will be the same." Her sobs grew louder as he moved deeper, inch by inch, stretching her as she fought and twisted. A strand of drool escaped her mouth, shining as it trailed towards the floor, and then he forced the rest of his cock in.

A scream escaped her, ending in a choked sob as she sputtered pleas, making the chains rattle when she moved her hands. Only the second cock she'd taken in her ass, it would still hurt plenty, and he was going to make her feel every bit of this violation. His brother may have been first, but he had rushed it — like he did everything — and so it would be *this* she remembered the most.

"You are not a person anymore, you're a slave. Property." Easing back, he thrust in a little harder, a little faster, ignoring the urge to tear her apart, focusing on every shiver, every whimper, every crumbling bit of hope.

But as much as she said she wanted to die — she would survive.

He would make sure of that.

"You are nothing more than a body for men to seek their pleasure in, to torment for their entertainment." Reaching forward, he caught her ponytail in his fist and wound it around to lift her head and pull her back on his cock, stretching her further. She choked out a pain-filled cry, eyes clenched tight as her fingers bent against the concrete. The sight of the gag between her lips, her tear-streaked cheeks, and the dark whip marks across her shoulders was perfect.

The customers will watch this over and over.

"I will take everything from you," his voice was strained because she squeezed his cock inside her. Rhythmic, twitching pulses in the tight sheath of her ass, but he was determined to make this last. To make her suffer more than she had with Marcus, to get her one step closer to breaking.

"It's up to you how long this lasts, slave." He fucked her a little harder, enjoying the throaty groan that slipped around the gag. "You choose when the training ends. So, how much can you take before you snap?"

TWELVE

Beth

Beth awoke with a jolt, panic and pain rushing through her, but when she tried to lift her hands they stopped short. The clatter of chain brought awareness of the cuffs on her wrists and ankles, but where was she?

Darkness.

Complete and total darkness.

Attempting to lift her head was almost futile, because the collar around her neck was attached to whatever she was lying on. Pressing her teeth into the narrow bit of rubber between her teeth she made herself swallow the pooling saliva.

Her heart was pounding, blood thumping inside her ears, but she tried her best to stay calm, to talk herself into sanity. Yet, something about the space around her felt stifling. Claustrophobic. Flaring her fingers out she brushed walls on either side of her body, and when she strained against the collar on her throat she managed to make her shoulder brush one side.

Oh God.

This is like a coffin. Is it a coffin? Did he bury me alive?

Horror movie scenarios flickered through her mind, and she couldn't control them. Couldn't stifle the thoughts as they made her panic. Whining against the gag, she pulled and kicked at the cuffs holding her down. Energy waning fast, she sobbed, trying not to choke on her drool as her nose clogged from the tears.

He said he wouldn't kill you.

He said it.

Somehow, that was a lifeline inside the nightmare. The promise of a psychopath holding her sanity together while she stared into the perfect darkness of the grave, pain creeping in at the edges of her awareness.

Her back and ass were alive with the marks from the whip, and every shift of her body reminded her of them. *That* had been worse than she'd imagined. Each strike of the sleek leather felt like it had torn skin and muscle, but she was quite sure she hadn't bled. She would have felt that, right?

Right?

The whimper echoed back too close, rebounding off a surface much nearer than she wanted to imagine. Visuals of being trapped in a fucking coffin were spinning around inside her head as she pictured that asshole with his stone-cold eyes shoveling dirt atop it.

Burying her alive.

Suddenly, it was too hard to breathe. Lungs cramping, tightening inside her ribcage, and she stretched her mouth wider than the gag so she could swallow more air. Strange, high-pitched noises were leaving her on every frenzied exhale, and she couldn't stop them.

Please let me out of here.

Please.

Rolling her head and eyes as much as she could she tried to search for light, for any hint, but there wasn't a shred. Nothing. Just darkness and a stifling warmth that made her question how much she was re-breathing her own air.

Am I light headed?

Is that from the panicked breathing or a lack of oxygen?

A scream ripped out of her, and she fought the restraints desperately, bucking her hips, twisting and pulling — but it was no use. She was just using more of the air struggling, and as the tears rolled from the edges of her eyes, tumbling into her hair, she forced herself to be still. To hold her breath, and then let it out as slow as possible. Gasping air in was an instinct, but she struggled to slow it too.

In and out.

Slow and even.

Where the fuck am I?

She remembered the whipping, remembered him fucking her ass slowly, the pain of it, the strain of the chains and the position... and then he had finished. *Right?*

Her thoughts grew thick at that point, muddy and sticky, and she wished anything in her life made sense. If it made sense she could understand where the fuck she was, but everything in her world was a nightmare. An incongruent horror show that seemed to have no end in sight.

How much can you take before you snap?

He had asked her that question again, and then he'd pressed her to the concrete with his cock still in her ass. Fucking her, he had asked it again, and again, and then his hand had come around her throat.

Unconscious.

That's what he'd done, he had choked her until she'd passed out — and then he'd apparently put her in a coffin. Beth whimpered, not sure if she wanted to die, or wanted to live, but she wanted *this* to stop.

'Please let me out, please. I'm sorry, I'm sorry…' The words were garbled, but she still tried to say them, to make them clear around the gag. Swallowing the saliva, she tried again, saying it louder, and then she strained her ears, listening for anything. Any sounds at all.

Silence.

Except for her breathing, and the dull clank of metal on metal whenever one of her limbs twitched. She had told him to just kill her, but she had hoped for a quick death, not suffocating or starving in a box.

Is that his plan?

More horror movie shit.

It was ridiculous, he wouldn't do it like this. Not in the dark. Not in this infinite darkness where none of those fucking cameras could watch her suffer. He'd do it with a knife out in the open, in that concrete room where there was already a drain to wash the evidence away. Or he'd electrocute her, because he liked electricity in all its forms.

Cattle prods, and electric batons, and devious boxes that rushed electricity into numerous devices that he'd pressed inside her and attached to her skin. It wouldn't be like this.

I won't die like this. I won't.

———

"AGH!" She woke up to the pressure of fingers deep inside her, stretching her, but the light was too bright to see. Whining she tried to tilt her hips away, but another finger joined the others and she screamed — was that four fingers? Was he trying to put his fucking fist inside her?

"STOP!" The word left her lips and she realized she could speak. The gag was gone. Ignoring the pain between her thighs she forced her eyes to pry open, wincing past the bright lights to make her eyes adjust.

Fingers spread and she groaned out her pain, clenching her teeth against the cry as she pulled at the cuffs. Still tied down, thighs spread just enough that she couldn't stop this.

"*Please*, fuck, please stop!"

"What do you say, slave?" It was him. He was above her, inside her, hurting her. *Again.*

"Oh God," she whispered, and then his fingers pushed deeper, knuckles stretching her cunt. That was the word he used, and it was the only one her mind would grasp as another torrent of pain shot through her. *Too much, too fucking much.*

"You know what you need to say. Say it and I will stop."

The bastard punctuated his statement by forcing his fingers a little farther in. He was tearing her, he had to be. The pain made her spine shiver, made her back arch, but her eyes slowly focused despite the tears blurring the edges.

He had one hand braced on something above her, something above the... drawer... she lay inside. That was it, she was in a drawer. A huge fucking drawer, with restraints. Turning her head, she saw the metal lining she lay on, the dark hole inside where she had been trapped. A gasp ripped from her lungs as pain spiked again, a whine as her whole body tensed with the stretch of four fingers forcing her wide, and then he slid back just enough to let her breathe. "Please!" she begged.

"Say it."

Master. Master. Master.

The only word he wanted. What would it mean to say it? What would he do if she did?

"You are going to suffer until you say it. I want you to understand that." His hand grabbed her jaw, and then his fingers left her cunt completely only to be forced into her mouth. Stretching her lips wide with the tang of her own taste — *when had she grown wet?*

He released her, and the last thing she saw was a blur of lights in the ceiling and his empty expression as he pushed the drawer shut and darkness overwhelmed her. Sore and whimpering she screamed for him to come back, but she didn't use the word.

There really was a magic word, but would using it be a blessing or a curse?

Drawer open.

The freezing spray of water hit her skin and she gasped, too stunned to scream, but then she remembered her thirst. Desperate for the water she kept her mouth obscenely open, swallowed as often as she could, fighting the urge to shiver and clench her teeth.

Then came the baton. Loud, electric zaps that had her convulsing on the metal tray in short bursts. Pain thundered through exhausted nerves, but all she wanted was the water back.

Still thirsty.

She hadn't been able to scream, or beg, in so long. Throat too dry, too raw from screaming in the damn drawer.

"Say it." His words buzzed in her ears, humming like the lingering vibration of the shocks. Wincing, she tried to look at him, to pull his image into focus, but he was backlit by bright lights and he was nothing more than a shadow. A pit of darkness.

"Say it or you go back in, slave."

Another zap, another groan, but all she wanted to ask for was the water. Even cold and biting, she didn't care. Just… "Water?" she croaked.

"Wrong answer."

The drawer slammed shut, rocking her body against the cuffs, and she flinched, tried to collect her thoughts into something not chaotic — but nothing worked.

Thirsty. I'm so thirsty.

Beth's world slid again. Hours, days in darkness, she didn't know how much time had passed. He hadn't fed her, twice he had sprayed her with water, and she had tried to swallow as much as she could, even as it stung her eyes and nose. Another he had used a short, leather thing on her flesh, striking and making her scream weakly as he hurt her. Another had been confusing, she had been sure she had seen two people, and then he had given her a shot — or it had felt like a shot — she couldn't remember.

Everything was fractured.

Something clicked and then he lifted her head, one fist buried in her hair, and the other pressed a glass to her lips. *Water*. It was the best thing she'd ever tasted, and she swallowed, and swallowed, feeling it wash into her empty stomach.

She wanted to thank him, wanted to be grateful, but then he took it away, and there was another loud *clank*, and she slid in a new direction. Towards him, his fist in her hair pulling her, but she still couldn't lift her arms and legs.

Blurry eyes opening, she saw the glass of water atop the cabinet where her drawer was, and then he released her head and it dropped. Too weak to fight him, too weak to lift it, too weak to turn away when he unbuttoned his pants and slid the zipper down.

His cock from this angle looked larger, and when he tapped her cheek and said, "Open," she obeyed without thinking. Fingers slipped into her mouth first, and she sucked, desperate for water, to make him happy, but he didn't say anything else as he slid them free and replaced them with his cock. Her jaw stretched, lips folding over teeth as he pushed in slowly, a heady groan from above.

Hitting the back of her throat meant little at this angle, but he paused enough to give her one short breath before he thrust forward, into the channel that cut off her air and made her choke. Sliding back, she coughed, sputtered, and then he forced his cock deep again, holding still with her nose against his balls.

Property.

A set of holes.

It was all true, that's what she felt like in this moment. Bound, unable to fight back, unable to struggle, no energy to be defiant and brave. He started to move, slowly at first, almost all the way out, letting her breathe, before plunging deep once more.

Catching on to the rhythm, she measured her breaths, and as his pace increased she had less and less air, until finally he was holding himself in her throat for longer and longer as she swallowed around his cock. Struggling weakly, twisting against the cuffs as she silently begged to breathe. He was fucking her throat, using her brutally, and the ache was getting worse the longer he continued.

Stop?

Such a useless word. It didn't do anything. Why had she ever even learned it? If someone wanted to ignore it, they did. Whether it was running a stop sign, or whipping someone, or fucking their throat — what did *stop* mean if it meant nothing?

Her mind was growing hazier, the fog thicker, and she felt numb as he worked in and out of her mouth, barely a snippet of air allowed on some of the harder thrusts that required him to pull back a little further. Throat on fire, tears burning her eyes, she felt his hand wrap around her throat and squeeze.

Is this it? Is this when he kills me?

Instead of death, she felt him come before she tasted it. Heard his low groan, felt his grip tighten across her neck, and then she was choking. As soon as he pulled out, her stomach emptied, and she heard him curse.

Still choking, she turned her head, but air wouldn't come.

Metallic clangs echoed like they were coming down a long hallway, and then her world turned again, and she was gone.

THIRTEEN

Beth

_____

Master.

You will call me Master.

There will be no freedom, no escape. You will call me Master, and then you will be sold to someone new, and then you will call him Master. That is your future. Accept it. Say it.

Words invaded her mind. His words. Digging in like burrowing worms until they felt like they had always been there. A permanent fixture in her head. An absolute truth. She fought them through the haze, pushed back as hard as she could, but they were there, and she was so tired.

It was a choice. One of the only choices she had left in this hell but making it would be worse than dying. It would be the death of her mind. The death of her self.

Saying it would finally make the first rule true — *I am not my own. I am property.*

The world around her felt distant, but she knew she was sitting up slightly, on a hard surface, which couldn't be the drawer. She had been held flat inside that hole. Getting her eyes open took too much effort, they felt swollen, the light burned, but finally she saw white, and dark gray walls.

A bathtub. She was in the bathroom, propped up in the oversized tub, with its angled side, and there was a large towel draped over her skin. No restraints here but, as she looked around, she saw a glass of water set on the edge and she grabbed it, spilling a little as she swallowed past an aching throat.

"Of course she's alive, I don't kill slaves." His voice came from the bedroom, speaking to someone.

Was the other one back? Beth strained to listen, to clear her mind enough to focus, but there was no other voice.

"The IV took care of that, and I thought we agreed you would not interfere." He was so calm, so empty, but she looked down at her arms, finding a pair of small, dark spots in the crook of her elbow.

He'd given her an IV. To keep her alive.

He wouldn't *allow* her to die.

Putting the glass down, she brushed the dots, traced the splotch of a bruise around them, and then she moved her fingers to her bruised wrist. Darker than before the whipping, before the drawer.

A shadow made her eyes lift, and he was there in the doorway. Dressed in a pristine pale button-down shirt, dark slacks, his shining shoes. He was holding the phone to his ear as his eyes moved over her, but there was something new in his expression.

Something terrifying.

There was a hint of anger narrowing his gaze, lowering his brows just a fraction, but as small as it was... it was still more expression than she'd seen out of him beyond his strange smiles.

His jaw twitched, and then he turned away, and a moment later she heard the door shut.

Anthony

"You just *had* to have this one, didn't you? Had to have the blonde California girl no matter what I said." Marcus was ranting, but Anthony's own temper was breaking through the cold he always felt. A rare occurrence.

"We both saw her on the beach, she drew *both* of our eyes. Do not pretend I made this decision on my own." Pacing the hallway, he forced a deep breath into his lungs.

"I told you I needed to follow her, needed to watch her, *you* put her on the fucking list as soon as you found out her name!"

"I've been taking girls for years without your assessment of their submissive traits, and there has never been an issue." Anthony felt his fingers form a fist, reassured that he'd turned off all the cameras so that Marcus couldn't see his reaction. He needed to get this back under control, needed to get *her* under control.

"You could have given me a fucking week!"

"We both agreed that having this operation offline for the duration of your house preparation would be fiscally irresponsible, and you needed to go North." Keeping his voice steady wasn't a challenge, it was the irritation moving through his veins that was troubling.

"Then you could have picked another name off the goddamn list, Anthony! ANY fucking name, it didn't have to be her!" Marcus shouted, and the volume of it was bothering him more than usual, getting under his skin faster.

He hated it.

"She was the highest potential profit on the list based on customer feedback."

"Well, now you have her! Your *high potential profit* cunt. So, what the fuck are you going to do with her?" Another slam of something from his end of the line. Marcus was breaking things, and for a moment Anthony wondered if that would help ease these strange sensations making his fist tighten, his jaw clench.

What would he do with her?

The problem wasn't a lack of ideas, he had too many things he wanted to do to her. Too many punishments in mind, each more severe than the last — but he didn't want to kill her. He *never* killed them.

For a time, the girl's defiance had been entertaining, so much better than the more fragile responses of others they had taken. The quick slide into constant crying, fear. This one had felt like a challenge at first, and he had enjoyed pushing her, bending her further and further, making her suffer.

But, by this point, every other girl had called him Master. By this point they were desperate to please him. Working on their submission, their behavior, learning to be perfect dolls as he erased their sense of self one punishment at a time.

It was why he'd used the drawer. Kept her in it for days, except for the brief interlude when he'd drugged her and hydrated her to avoid seizures, to ensure her kidneys wouldn't shut down.

The drawer should have worked.

The drawer *always* worked.

Yet, she had refused to say the simple word.

Anthony despised it when things didn't work the way they were supposed to, and this slut was clearly malfunctioning. The drawer should have shattered her mind, left her hopeless and begging — and she *had* begged, and cried, looking pretty and desolate on the tiny night vision cameras — but each time he had pulled her out, she had defied him.

"I'm going to break her," he finally answered.

Marcus laughed, broke something else, cursed. "How the fuck do you plan to do that Anthony? No girl has ever lasted this long without submitting, and you think you can fully break her?"

"Yes." It was a quick response, almost too quick. He hadn't even thought it through.

Was this his pride showing?

"HOW?" His brother yelled the word, and Anthony tilted his head, cracking the vertebrae in his neck in an effort to relax the tensing muscles.

"She thinks she wants to die… I plan to give her a taste."

"A taste of *dying*? What the fuck does that mean?" Marcus was muttering curses, randomly shouting in his rage, but Anthony's mind was finally clearing. A plan forming, organized and purposeful.

"Watch and see. I will let her recover for a day or so, allow her enough strength so that she can be aware, and then I will break her."

"What if this fails too, Anthony? What will you do with her?" There was a thread of concern there, a nervousness in his brother's voice, and it made Anthony smile.

"I'll destroy her."

FOURTEEN

Beth

Soup and sleep.

Water and rest.

The bed was soft, warm, an extra blanket atop the normal sheet. He hadn't touched her since he had pulled her from the bathtub and settled her here, and she had only left the cocoon she'd created to use the bathroom.

But everything still hurt.

Beth had explored the whip marks in the mirror, stared into the face that used to be so familiar, but now it had changed. *She* had changed. Dark circles under dull, bloodshot brown eyes. Cheekbones sharper, lips chapped and dry. It wasn't her, she felt disconnected from the girl in the mirror, didn't *want* to be her.

He was tearing her apart. More than just physically, the worst of the damage was inside. The parts she could only get a glimpse of when she had the courage to stare into her own eyes — but she couldn't maintain it for long. It hurt too much.

The last blow was the tattoo on the inside of her hip. A small thing. From what she could tell it was a 'W' with a crown atop it, underlined with a slash. Dark ink embedded in her skin, still tender to the touch, and she knew he had done it while she had been in the drawer. The time he had drugged her, given her the IV fluids.

What else had he done while she was unconscious?

Roaming her body with her fingers, she had explored every inch. Wound them under the collar, plucking at the small padlock that never budged. She was not as sore between her thighs, and the whip marks simply felt like bruises, although they hurt more than the ones on her wrists and ankles. There was nothing else that was new, no other tattoos, just a body that didn't feel like hers.

A body she wasn't sure she wanted to hold onto anymore.

The other one had claimed she had choices. At the time those choices had felt numerous, so many little battles of wills — some won, some lost — but now there was only one left. It was the only thing that mattered anymore.

He wanted her mind like he had taken her body.

But she would die before she gave it to him.

FIFTEEN

Beth

———

At least two days had passed in silence.

Every time he came to the room to leave a tray, or pick up another, she simply watched him. He would look at her too, that same analytical stare from the first night, except there were no strange smiles now.

No words. No demands. No threats.

Nothing except a quick exchange of gazes... which was fine with her. She didn't want to talk to the monster.

Beth felt stronger, her head clearer. Finally hydrated, and nourished, and well-slept. It seemed that all she did was sleep, but she needed it. The unconsciousness in the drawer, and all the other times, had never felt like sleep — there had been no dreams — but now she was dreaming.

Scattered, whirlwind dreams of familiar voices. Flashes of friendly faces, her family. In one she was simply driving and listening to music, on one of the coastal highways with the sun glinting off the ocean.

It had been simple and peaceful. No nightmares.

But it wasn't like her mind needed to create nightmares when she always awoke in hell, always awoke locked in the same room, in the same house, with the same man — and she knew this strange peace wouldn't last.

He was waiting for something.

Anthony

The camera angle switched again, showing the flare of her blonde hair against the pillow, the shape of her body under the blankets. Tapping a few keys on the keyboard, he made the angle switch again, zooming in on her face.

Asleep.

His phone buzzed again, and he felt his shoulders tighten. It was another email. He knew it without checking. The customers were complaining, a few of them had offered to *assist* him with her, which had almost resulted in a hasty reply, but he had halted himself.

Patience was key, especially with the customers, but the general summary of their feedback was nothing but dissatisfaction.

Not only was she irritating him, now she was damaging their brand. So much money, and time, and energy building his reputation among these wealthy men across the globe. Getting them to trust him, to trust his security measures and his discretion.

She was ruining everything.

Anthony cracked his neck again, leaning closer to the screen where her face was formed in tiny pixels. The girl always kept the bathroom light on, and it meant she was still in color, albeit somewhat washed out — but he could see her face was fuller, that color had returned to her cheeks. She was more stable.

Stable enough to survive what he had planned.

Drumming his fingers on his desk, he felt another vibration from his phone and he swept it off the desk with a quick jerk of his arm. It clattered to the floor, lighting up, and he gradually became aware of the increased pace of his breaths.

Anger, stress — if he were capable of feeling those things, he was feeling them now. None of it processed right in his head, but he knew the signs. Had observed them in Marcus for decades, and extraordinary circumstances had summoned similar things in him before.

This girl was an extraordinary circumstance.

One that he was about to rectify permanently. And then everything would return to normal, the process would work again, customer expectations would be met, and the cold calm of his brain would be restored.

Drawing in a slow breath, he released it and pushed up from the desk. Calmly lifting the phone from the floor, he tucked it into his pocket and tugged his sleeves into place.

It was time to get his world back under control.

Walking to her room gave him enough time to solidify his expression into neutrality, to even out his breathing so that he was as composed as he needed to be to do this properly.

The act of unlocking and opening the door had woken her. Eyes open, she simply stared at him, unmoving, and he felt a much more familiar urge overtake the strange flickers he'd felt before. He was going to make her suffer, to tear out whatever shreds of hope she had left — and watching this one finally break was going to be the greatest enjoyment he'd had in years.

"Get up." They were the first words he'd said to her in days, but he had not expected her to obey. When she slid the blankets back, sitting up on the edge of the bed, it *almost* caught him off-guard.

Her lithe form stretched out as she stood, her legs steady, and he reached back to press in the code for the door, opening it wide.

"Come here." Anthony felt a hint of satisfaction when she walked towards him in careful steps, a passing taste of her obedience that he knew wouldn't last, so he grabbed onto the back of her collar. "Have you decided to submit?" he asked as he pushed her into the hall.

She stayed silent, but she didn't fight him as they walked towards the punishment room. Perhaps she felt it too, this inevitability of their interaction, the coming conclusion. When she was silent like this, pliant, he could almost imagine her becoming a good slave, but he knew her compliance wouldn't last.

Not when she saw what awaited her. Understood it.

Walking into the punishment room, the girl finally jerked against his grip. The new furniture in the center of the floor had her complete attention, and he allowed her a moment to stare. She would never discern its use — if she did, she'd start screaming. "Get on the table."

This time her obedience wavered. When he released her, she stood completely still. The snap of the door shutting made her muscles jump, and she was aware, coherent, but not moving. Not obeying.

Fisting the tangled mess of her hair, he forced her forward until they stood beside the shiny metal. Dark cuffs already installed and waiting for her, she whimpered quietly, and he could feel her leaning back from the table — as if that would stop him. "Up."

Increasing the strain, he pulled her onto it when she didn't obey. Normally, he'd punish her with a shock, but it was best not to distress her before he began, and it didn't take much effort to push her flat and then drag her down the table to strap her ankles into the cuffs.

When he looked at her again, her eyes were glued somewhere on the ceiling, head subtly moving from side to side like she was saying no. It brought a smile to his lips.

So quiet now, and soon there would be so much screaming.

Beth

Save your energy. Save your energy. Save it.

You won't win anyway.

It took more self-control than Beth thought she had, but she let him maneuver her body into place on the cold metal table. Cuffs at ankles and wrists brought back flashes of the drawer, but her collar wasn't attached to anything, and there was light. Plenty of light.

She was directly under the camera in the ceiling, unable to avoid staring into the dark, glass eye. People would see this, whatever it was, and she focused on the promise she'd made to herself.

No matter what he does, I won't give him my mind.

If he wanted an audience for this, then she was going to make sure he failed in front of them. It was the only choice left for her, the only shred of power, of control. The table shifted and she lifted her head to see him turning some kind of handle out of sight. As he continued, the end of the table started to rise, but the cuffs held her in place as the angle increased.

What the fuck is this?

When he finally stopped, she realized the incline wasn't severe, head slightly closer to the floor than her feet, but it was enough to make her uncomfortable. Then he was there beside the table, trailing his fingers over her stomach, between her breasts, catching her chin so that she had to look at him. "You know what I want you to say. Do you want to avoid all of this and just obey?"

"Fuck. You." Beth lifted her chin away from his touch as she enunciated each word, staring into those empty blue eyes that did nothing to hide the monster inside him. He was pure evil, a psychopath, and giving in wouldn't stop this — he had told her over and over that she was never getting free.

The bastard smiled. Satisfaction coating the razor-sharp edges of his expression, and despite her best efforts fear still bloomed in her stomach. "Since that vulgarity is your answer, we will begin."

He turned away, walking to the table against the wall as he unbuttoned one sleeve and rolled it up. The second sleeve was adjusted with quick jerks of his hand as he stared down at the metal table. It was almost empty except for a frosted pitcher, which he picked up along with a cloth. She twisted her head to keep him in her sight as he moved to the waterspout jutting from the concrete. The loud sound of the spray hitting the plastic made her swallow, trying to understand what he had planned.

Was he going to electrocute her again?

As soon as the water cut off, he raised his eyes to hers. "You only have one purpose, slave. You understand that, correct?"

"No," she spat, glaring at him, refusing to back down. *No matter what he does. No matter what.*

"It will be so fun to watch you break." His smile turned the fear into whirling blades in her belly, and she hated feeling so vulnerable, so weak, as he towered over her. Then he tilted the pitcher just enough to splash water onto her face. Clenching her eyes shut she shook it away, licking at the lingering drops on her lips before she returned to glaring at him.

"You're not going to break me. I'm not going to obey—" Cutting off her hissing rage with another little splash, he *tsk'd* as she jerked at the cuffs, blinking away the water from her eyes, muttering curses.

"I will admit that you have held on to your defiance longer than other girls I have taken, but what you fail to grasp is that *everyone* breaks, slave. There is a limit to what your mind can take... and today we are going to find it."

"No." Beth tried to sound confident, but the glint in his eyes promised violence. Pain. Suffering.

"Tell me, girl, do you know what waterboarding is?" The word made her still against the table. *Torture. That was torture, right?* He ran his fingers over her cheek, leaning closer. "No? Let me show you."

Suddenly, there was a cloth over her face, held down by his hand around her jaw, and then she felt the water. She tried to gasp, jerking at the cuffs, but water poured into her nose and mouth. No air. Fabric stuck to her skin, blocking everything as he continued to pour.

Oh God, I'm drowning.

As soon as the water stopped, he pulled the cloth away and she choked, spitting water as she turned her head to the side, lifting her shoulders as much as possible to force it out so she could haul in a ragged breath. More violent coughs, and then his hand landed on her chest and slammed her back to the table. Eyes and nose burning, lungs aching, panic rising — he stared at her like an insect. Like prey. "I'm sure you understand the situation now. Will you address me properly?"

Hauling air into her lungs, she clenched her fists, driving her nails into her palms. "You're an asshole. A monster! A fucking rap—" The wet cloth was back over her face in an instant, his hard grip molding it to her face, making her jaw ache, and then the water came again.

She tried to scream, but breathed water instead, and her body convulsed, choked, alarm bells ringing in her body. *Dying. Can't breathe. He's going to kill me.*

Bright lights blinded her as she coughed violently, almost heaving as water flooded out of her nose, lungs convulsing to force out more. Her ears were ringing, but his voice came in loud and clear, "Say it."

Wheezing in air, she coughed again, and shook her head slowly. "Fuck you," she whispered, voice scratchy and strained.

His jaw clenched, a muscle twitching in his neck, and then he backhanded her. Pain exploded in her cheek, and she yelped, couldn't stop the cry. The cloth returned then, just as she tried to refill her lungs, and she was drowning again. Choking on screams until her heels kicked at the table, arms desperate to rip free of the cuffs, but there was no escape. Instinct demanded she try to breathe, but there was only water, and she fought it, fought it until even with her lips pressed closed her brain tried to draw breath through her nose.

Anthony

The girl convulsed, chest jerking, breasts bouncing as he counted in his head. *Nineteen, twenty, twenty-one… twenty-two.* Finally he lifted the pitcher upright, moving the cloth free, and water spouted out of her like a fountain. Her first effective cough, and he watched her breathe. *One, two…* "Say it, slave."

Her body jerked violently, struggling against the cuffs, and then she screamed. It was filled with rage, fury, and he silenced her with the cloth, holding it down as he poured the last of the water in the pitcher over her face slowly.

The jingling sound of the cuffs at her wrists and ankles, the muffled, guttural groans in her chest, all of it distracted him from the fact that he hadn't counted.

Don't kill her.

The last of the pitcher emptied, and Anthony pulled the cloth away. She threw up water, shoulder lifting as she turned to the side and expelled a torrent onto the table and floor. None of it bothered him. That was what this room was for — easy clean up — and she hadn't hit him with any of it.

Still, he needed her able to respond. Needed her alive.

Marcus would be watching. As soon as he had turned the cameras back on, everyone had received the alert, including his wayward brother.

Which meant he needed to control this situation. Taking the pitcher back to the faucet, he filled it, refusing to even look at her as he listened to the haggard breaths, the wheezing, and then she screamed again. Raw and desperate.

A living thing wanting to stay alive.

"Say it," he demanded as he turned back towards her, gripping the cloth tight in his fist until he felt rivulets streaming between his fingers.

Her brown eyes met his as her ribs jerked with another cough. "*No.* Just kill me."

A smile twitched at his lips, cock hardening in his pants, urging him to make her submit. To break her until she was nothing more than a mindless doll, an object, a slave.

She didn't want to die, and he was going to prove it to her.

"Take a breath," he warned her a split second before he blocked her nose and mouth with the soaked cloth, holding it taut to her cheeks as he started to pour again. *Thirty seconds this time.*

Beth

Beth wanted to let go, wanted to breathe the water deep and end this nightmare, but her fucking body wouldn't let her. Her mind fought her, overruled her, flooded her system with adrenaline and raw panic until she was fighting the cuffs and choking on water as her useless lungs sought air.

And then the bastard gave it to her, lifted the cloth so she could drive out the water with painful convulsions, loud, strangled sounds, pulling oxygen back in that did nothing more than drag this hell out a little longer.

Whimpers were slipping from her, tears burning her eyes, but at least they were invisible amidst all of the water.

"How much more can you take?" he asked, one of his favorite questions, and she refused to look at him. Instead, she stared at the ceiling, occasionally racked by coughs as her lungs found a new pocket of water. "Say it, slut. Now."

A new edge to his voice. Hard and cold as steel.

The automaton was angry, which meant she was winning.

Dying, but winning.

Cloth and water returned, and she tried to breathe it in, to finally die, but she choked instead. And with the choking came more panic, more automatic responses, her body keeping her alive despite her best efforts — and with the jerking of her lungs, the feeling of drowning, came so much pain. Everything burned, her head spun, and she was screaming, sobbing as he pulled back again and her body emptied as much of the water as it could.

Refusing to die. Refusing to end this.

The broken wail that left her was all self-pity, because the rage was leaving her with every second she spent without air. Even when he wrenched her head back by her hair, ice cold eyes burning above hers, she barely had the energy to hate him.

"Say. It," he hissed into her face, but all she did was cough. Sputtering water from bruised lungs. In the haze of her wheezing breaths, the grunt as he shoved her head to the side — Beth could hear a dull, patterned vibration. But then it was gone, replaced with the cloth, the deafening sound of water smothering her, drowning her.

Head swimming, she couldn't coordinate thoughts. Everything narrowed down to the urge to breathe, to the feel of water forcing its way up her nose and into her throat. No way to stop it, even as her body jerked weakly, mindless whimpers and cries broken by desperate choking.

Air came again, but only after she'd heaved what felt like a gallon out of her nose and mouth. Her breaths were hitched, almost every indrawn breath resulting in a wracking cough that only exhausted her further.

There was a dull beep, and she opened her eyes, the blurry shape of him coming into view near the other table. He had set the pitcher down, and he was talking. "—not your concern. She will live."

Those words pried something loose inside her, something important, something foundational that had been holding other things together. Something she'd been standing on as she fought to win against him. Whatever it was, it had been holding her, and when it snapped, everything else… shifted. Tumbled. And there was only the avalanche. Absolute chaos took over inside what was left of her mind as he moved back towards her, carrying the pitcher in one hand, a cell phone pressed to his ear in the other. A flicker of thought reminded her that she should be afraid, but it was only a second before it slipped away, left her staring at pale blue eyes almost glowing with anger.

"Watch and see," he hissed, and then the phone was gone, a dull beep and then the cloth was back.

Drenched in black, suffocating, Beth wanted to breathe. She just wanted to breathe, wanted to turn away from the water so she could find air. Thoughts were short-circuiting, tumbling on half-finished cycles but still repeating.

You have to win.

Are you winning?

Win. Don't give in. Win.

A convulsion shook her, lungs choking on water. The cloth was gone, she could see light, but air couldn't get past the water. Too much of it, filling her mouth, running out of her nose, burning her eyes. Everything felt so far away, but the pain was still close. Prying between her ribs like a monster trying to rip her chest open. Lungs on fire.

On fire underwater.

How was I supposed to win again?

"Say it. Now. Say it now, slave. Call me Master!" The man's voice was close, his warm exhale brushing over the cool flesh of her cheek, and as his hand tightened over her throat one of her hands tried to lift.

Stop…

A metal *clank* held her arm in place. No way to stop the tightening grip, the throaty whimper as air squeaked out of her lungs. Then came the soaked cloth, another river of water.

Drowning.

It was supposed to be peaceful, right?

But it wasn't. That was a lie. The panic pulled her up from the edge of the abyss, kept her out of the peace as her heart raced, as her body twisted, kicked. Another painful eruption of water, endless, then, after one breath of air, she was under the cloth once more.

Water came again. Water washed inside, swelled against the broken foundation inside her, the thing that was so important, the thing she'd held onto… and swept it away.

All of it.

Gone. Nothingness. The thing was important, so important, but it was splintering, and there wasn't enough left to know what was missing — what had been taken.

It was just gone.

Sunk to the bottom, somewhere far out of reach. Far away, under the water.

Just like she was.

Lost.

Empty.

Free.

SIXTEEN

Anthony

───────────

Anthony leaned against the wall, breathing hard, staring at the almost perfectly still figure of the girl on the shining metal. A weak cough shook her, water running from the side of her mouth, her eyes unfocused on the ceiling.

For a moment he'd been sure that he had killed her, and then he had forced her head to the side, dropped the pitcher and lifted her shoulder. Holding her in place until biology took over and water had poured out. A quiet, meek gasp, another cough, a gagging heave, more water, and then she'd been limp.

Vacant.

Barely perceptible breaths expanding her ribs, and he had stepped back.

Anger still flickered somewhere in him. At least, the closest thing he could feel to it… because she hadn't said the word.

She'd broken first.

His phone vibrated repeatedly in his pocket, but Marcus would have to wait. Collecting himself, storing the strange flashes of rage away in his mind, he pushed away from the wall and approached her.

No reaction, no increase in breaths, no sudden twitch to make her limbs fight the cuffs.

Nothing.

Turning the handle at the end of the table, he lowered it flat again. It had been tilted at exactly twenty-five degrees. He had never passed thirty seconds on the waterboarding. Yet, the girl was blank.

Walking to the head of the table, he leaned over her, bracing one hand on the other side of her so he was directly in her line of sight. Brown eyes stared straight through him, lips parted as air rattled its way into her lungs and whispered its way back out.

Fuck.

He despised expletives, but there was no other internal reaction that fit this moment. The girl was supposed to submit, to break enough to call him Master, to accept her position — she wasn't supposed to be like *this*.

Anthony caught her chin in his fingers, squeezing hard enough to bruise, but all it earned was a blink. A slow flutter of damp eyelashes.

"Speak, slave." It was a command. Everything in his tone demanded an answer, the pain he delivered with the force of his grip was irrefutable, but the girl didn't even react.

Standing upright again, he slapped her hard. Her head whipped to the side... and stayed. Staring at the opposite wall, breaths still disturbingly slow as the pink outlines of his fingers formed on her skin.

Fuck.

Another set of vibrations came from the phone in his pocket, and he glanced up at the camera in the ceiling and shook his head once. The buzzing stopped a second later.

He needed to think. Something *other* than useless expletives.

The girl was broken, that was undeniable. She *might* come back in a week or two. A month. And he had customers who would pay extra for the opportunity to do things to her in this state — they might even wake her up. Bring her back from this vacant state, to be useful enough to sell to one of his traditional clients.

If not…

Anthony sighed and looked her over. She hadn't lifted her face back towards the ceiling, had not moved at all as far as he could tell. Even her hands were open, palms towards the ceiling like a doll.

If he couldn't get her responsive, couldn't form her into any kind of obedience, then there were always people who didn't care about things like that. They did not pay as well, there was no acclaim in selling a girl to those parts of the world, but it was *some* profit.

And if she wouldn't respond, then there was no other use for her.

Broken dolls simply weren't entertaining.

Epilogue

ANTHONY

Four Weeks Later

Anthony sat in front of the fire, his shoes on the leather ottoman to enjoy the warmth as he tapped out replies to emails.

The business never stopped.

Customers in almost every time zone across the globe. So much hunger. So many dark wishes to be fulfilled.

A call interrupted his email screen, and he rejected Marcus so that he could finish typing. More confirmations that his feed would be online again *soon*... there were just so many decisions to make. What would the customers want from him now? What would the customers allow him to do... and keep paying?

The girl, *Beth*, had opened so many new avenues, and she had no idea about it. Marcus' new slave was already coming like a porn star on command, even though she cried whenever they finished. Entertaining? Yes. Effective? That was yet to be determined.

Most of their customers were not interested in pleasing the slaves they purchased. That relationship was decidedly inverse, which was what Marcus failed to understand. Slaves should seek to please their Master, regardless of any benefits they received from the interaction. Whether it be food, or comfort, or pleasure.

Marcus was training girls to expect pleasure, and that would eventually be disastrous.

Finishing his email, he assured another long-term customer that his feed would continue soon. Even tempted him with the promise of new recordings.

Then another interruption, more buzzing. He was calling again. Tapping the *answer* button, Anthony held the phone to his ear. "Yes?"

"How is she?" The abrupt question made him smile, leaning over to wake up the tablet so he could watch her on the internal camera feed.

"Busy."

"What the fuck does that mean?" Marcus snapped.

"She's with a guest."

"You're running a fucking whorehouse now? Is that the deal?" His brother growled on the other end of the line, and Anthony let him continue his rambling. "This is ridiculous. You said you could fix her."

"I *am* fixing her, Marcus. This is what will wake her up." *Or it wouldn't.* But that conversation would only make his brother more irritable, and therefore more irritating.

"Who the fuck do you have over there? Sam?"

"No, Sam is not here." *Today.* "And I'm sure you understand that discretion is important to our customers. It is not necessary for you to know, so you don't need to."

"That's bullshit! We're supposed to be partners, and you told me you'd fix Beth. Handing her over to your friends isn't fucking fixing her!"

"First, these are *customers*, not friends. Don't be ridiculous." Anthony reached for the glass of sherry and took a small sip, savoring it before he continued. "Second, we may be partners in this enterprise, but how I handle my slaves is my business. I haven't called you to ask about the number of orgasms you've given that slut in your house, have I?"

"At least my slave isn't catatonic."

Shrugging, Anthony glanced at the tablet again. The customer had her on the bed, knees bent towards her shoulders as he fucked her hard. Of course, the girl was unresponsive, staring off toward one wall, but it didn't seem to dissuade the man atop her at all — which was promising. *Very* promising. "My slave is doing just fine, and while I adjust her behavioral issues, I plan to take another one."

"What?" Marcus growled.

"She takes almost no supervision and, while she is adjusting, I may as well produce another more amicable slave." Anthony lifted the tablet and switched camera angles so that he could see the girl's empty eyes as she rocked against the bedding.

Was she even aware of the man inside her? Had she felt the flogger? The cane?

"You can't be serious." His brother laughed as he spoke, and Anthony dropped the tablet from his view. The girl had become boring as soon as she'd stopped responding, stopped fighting. There was no fun in fucking her when she didn't scream, or cry. It was like masturbating with a warm doll — effective, but not satisfying.

"Of course, I'm serious. You have your business, and I have mine."

"Well, *your* business isn't done. You haven't sold Beth."

"I can sell her today, if you'd like?" Anthony offered, and reveled in the growl that came across the line.

"Where? Your friends in South Asia?"

"Again, they are business contacts, not *friends*, Marcus. And yes, I have contacts in Thailand who would love to add a pretty little blonde to their offerings." The idea was tempting, it would take an email, then a phone call, and she'd be out of his house.

He would just need to finish working through the list of customers who had wanted to try her first.

"You can't sell her like that, Anthony." Marcus huffed. "She's not even *there*. You didn't break her, you shattered her. Fuck, you have to feed her! Those assholes in Thailand won't do that, you might as well kill her."

"I don't kill slaves."

"*Right*. You just ruin them." Laughing, low and bitter, Marcus leaked pride into his voice. "At least I've got this one almost ready to go so our customers don't leave and go to some other operation."

"Your first auction, already? It hasn't even been three

weeks. Are you sure you want to bet before you've even done the kitchen test?" Anthony lifted the tablet to switch to Marcus' feed. The small, dark haired girl was in his punishment room, complete with his collection of BDSM-style furniture and tools.

"She'll pass."

"We'll see," Anthony answered, but Marcus laughed again.

"Beth didn't pass."

Anthony smiled slowly, tapping until her room showed on the feed again. His customer was finished, and she was lying flat on the bed, legs slightly parted. "I never tried the test, Marcus. That's the difference here. I know what they are ready for, your pride blinds you."

"Fuck you."

"No, I'm not interested in incest, but I'm sure your whore could use another few orgasms to *ready* her for the kitchen test." He smiled, tapping his fingers against the glass of sherry. "Maybe I'll come and help with it."

"I don't want you here," Marcus hissed.

"Oh, but that's not really your choice, is it?" Waiting, Anthony turned back to the feed of the dark-haired girl. Sated and asleep. *She* was responsive, even though she no longer fought Marcus. But she would probably fight him. Call out for his brother, call out *Master* hoping to be saved, but Marcus would never interrupt him. He'd let him take her, let him hurt her so that she learned what her future could be. So that she could accept it.

"Erin isn't ready, yet."

"Then she isn't ready for the kitchen test either, is she, Marcus?" He traced the girl's figure on the screen, waiting.

"Maybe next week. I'll check on Beth later." With that, Marcus ended the call, and Anthony set the phone down, allowing his brother a few more days with his first girl in the new house.

It wasn't like he had *nothing* to entertain him. Beth was still a set of holes, a broken doll that he could do what he wanted with, and as soon as his customer gave his feedback and left, Anthony could enjoy himself.

A knock sounded at the door, and he stood to let the man inside.

Once he was gone, he could stand Beth in the shower and wash her clean. It would be easy. She stood when directed, bent in the ways he made her. Just like a doll. And then he could take her to the living room and play with her as he relaxed — they had only made so much progress on her gag reflex, and it would be another marketable component if he could get her to the point where she took a cock down her throat without gagging quite so loudly.

Anything to get more money out of his Thai contacts when he finally got rid of her.

Then, Anthony would need to look at the list of potentials and choose who he'd entertain himself with next. Maybe this time he'd narrow the customer list, keep only the more hardcore customers… the ones who liked it when he hurt them. Made them suffer.

Marcus could have the pleasure, the companionship, the gentility.

Anthony would handle the destruction.

It had always been a talent.

The End

End Note

Need a minute? I understand, lovely. I'll wait.

. . .

Okay, now that you've read Beth's history, I want to hear what you think. Talk about it in the Dark Haven group with me, or send me an email, or chat with me. Reach out as you process Marcus and Anthony in a new light. I can almost guarantee if you go back and read 'Security Binds Her' now you'll listen to their conversations in a much different way.

So, what's next? Well, I plan to continue Beth's story, and like always… give her a happy ending. Yes, I know who her hero will be, and *yes*, you've already met him in the Thalia series. No, I will not tell you who it is. The good news is that I plan to tell their story in a duet, which (I'm sure you can tell) is going to require a good deal of healing. If you've read the end of the Thalia series, you'll remember hearing from Beth in 'Tying the Knot'… and you'll probably remember just how much healing she has to do.

It's going to be a rough, heart-wrenching road, but I'm hoping you'll take it with me, lovelies. She deserves it, right?

Now, usually this is the place I'd say that I hope you enjoyed the book, but... that phrasing just doesn't seem appropriate here. Instead, I'll just answer the question that might be tingling in your minds.

Was this the darkest I could go?

Answer? *No. (sorry?)*

You may have noticed that Anthony has his own odd little code of ethics, and while the plan for this story was originally to take the chains off, I still have to stay true to the characters. Since the boxset went so well, and there seem to be enough dark and twisted fans out there for the authors who were involved, we will likely do another one in the future, and for *that* one I'll really open the basement doors and let the demons play. I'll find you lovelies a villain that isn't quite so... restrained.

#cackles

Yeah, I'm fucked up, but I'm lucky enough to have all of you, and a bunch of wonderful friends who love me anyway. Can't wait to chat with you all about this!

Talk to you soon,

Jennifer Bene

About the Author

Jennifer Bene is a *USA Today* bestselling author of dangerously sexy and deviously dark romance. From BDSM, to Suspense, Dark Romance, and Thrillers—she writes it all. Always delivering a twisty, spine-tingling journey with the promise of a happily-ever-after.

Don't miss a release! Sign up for the newsletter to get new book alerts (and a free welcome book) at: http://jenniferbene.com/newsletter

You can find her online throughout social media with username @jbeneauthor and on her website: www.jenniferbene.com

Also by Jennifer Bene

The Thalia Series (Dark Romance)

Security Binds Her *(Thalia Book 1)*

Striking a Balance *(Thalia Book 2)*

Salvaged by Love *(Thalia Book 3)*

Tying the Knot *(Thalia Book 4)*

The Thalia Series: The Complete Collection

Dangerous Games Series (Dark Mafia Romance)

Early Sins *(A Dangerous Games Prequel)*

Lethal Sin *(Dangerous Games Book 1)*

Damaged Goods *(Dangerous Games Book 2)*

Fragile Ties Series (Dark Romance)

Destruction *(Fragile Ties Book 1)*

Inheritance *(Fragile Ties Book 2)*

Redemption *(Fragile Ties Book 3)*

The Beth Series (Dark Romance)

Breaking Beth *(Beth Book 1)*

Daughters of Eltera Series (Dark Fantasy Romance)

Fae *(Daughters of Eltera Book 1)*

Tara *(Daughters of Eltera Book 2)*

Standalone Dark Romance

Taken by the Enemy

Imperfect Monster

Corrupt Desires

The Rite

Deviant Attraction: A Dark and Dirty Collection

Reign of Ruin

Crazy Broken Love

Appearances in the Black Light Series (BDSM Romance)

Black Light: Exposed *(Black Light Series Book 2)*

Black Light: Valentine Roulette *(Black Light Series Book 3)*

Black Light: Roulette Redux *(Black Light Series Book 7)*

Black Light: Celebrity Roulette *(Black Light Series Book 12)*

Standalone BDSM Ménage Romance

The Invitation

Reunited

Printed in Great Britain
by Amazon